DEDICATION

Special thanks to my sons and their families for all the
encouragement and help they always give sharing their own excellent
knowledge in story work, and every success to my eldest son as his
new book is nearing completion.

Contents

The Mysteries of Rome and Intrigue

By
Robert Faulkner

MAPLE
PUBLISHERS

The Mysteries of Rome and Intrigue

Author: Robert Faulkner

Email ID: rgaj@hotmail.co.uk

ISBN 978-1-83538-865-5 (Paperback)

Book Cover design and Layout by:
White Magic Studios
www.whitemagicstudios.co.uk

Published by:
Maple Publishers
Fairbourne Drive, Atterbury,
Milton Keynes,
MK10 9RG, UK
www.maplepublishers.com

A CIP catalogue record for this title is available from the British Library.

Chapter 1

Athens

"Welcome back to Greece, Giorgio! You're looking well." "Thank you, Emilio, and it's good to see you again. It's been a while; you're looking fit and prosperous. This section obviously agrees with you. I'm sorry to hear it's your last tour, and possibly mine. Neither of us will suit the inactive lifestyle of a desk no matter how big it is."

"I agree, Giorgio, but I will have Lucia to organise my routine. Who will you have now? Anyway, come, we need to move you away from this busy place and all the tourists; Lucia, my aide, has booked you into your usual hotel suite. All your bags are cleared and in the car, which is waiting. We can talk there and on the way to your hotel, as we will be taking the scenic business route since it will be our last opportunity. Although you may need to visit one of our associates to advise them of our intentions and our requirements to this latest incident, other than that, I can show you where other establishments are now located. I am sure you will enjoy the route as it is one that various drivers have taken you on during your brief visits to dealing with assorted business types for working lunches."

"Emilio, we should always find time to enjoy the exquisite qualities and fine Grecian elegance of this city, which I might add we have both enjoyed on returning from the field." "All now sadly in the past, Giorgio. Lucia says this present crisis will need all your attention and mine. Sadly, my friend, our time is limited with all our hours pre-booked for the short time we are here in Athens. You will have to eat and socialise in-house, but you are used to living in hotels. And look, there your second home."

"True, and having read the abbreviated details of this visit, Emilio, I guessed as much. Although it means zero socialising, the upside of being in the office will give me chance to catch up on company procedures and protocols again. I shall have to abandon my rough practical ways of getting things done."

"Giorgio, it will be good for you to be back from external operations, and in the comparative safety of our armoured umbrella, away from the hazards you have recently experienced. Although, that shortcut through the old mine field, avoiding others, was a good move, and I know we have the training to walk on the tyre tracks, yet it's always a worry as one of the girls told me in D section."

"The joys of field work, Emilio."

"Maybe, Giorgio, but others will be glad to see you back safely. Lucia used to tell me you cannot be at sea for too long, even seabirds want to fly home in the end. Also, Giorgio, the hotel has had a face-lift and internal refit with more room refinements, better access and security, which reminds me to make you aware that claiming expenses has come under scrutiny again."

"Have you had more social extravagances, Emilio?"

"Not too many, but it is expected, when you are entertaining certain groups to gather information."

"It sounds plausible, Emilio."

We made our way to the hotel lift area.

"Giorgio, the hotel manager Andreus is coming over. We can thank him for listening to our security suggestions and feedback for extra facilities during our last social gathering."

The manager started greeting and talking.

"Giorgio, it is good to see you again. We have not seen you for a while. You have been enjoying the sun. Yes? We hope you will enjoy your stay with us again."

"Thank you, Andreus! It's good to see you too and the uplifting new style. It's much appreciated to see and hear about the additional changes we all agreed from our last social meeting."

"Thank you, Giorgio. It is still a well-remembered night, the band asked to be remembered if I should see you for an enjoyable time they had. I hope you will find everything satisfactory in your room, including our special complimentary baskets exclusive to the suite."

"Well, Giorgio, everything is to your satisfaction, and the room is how you remember. Exactly how I remember it, even with all the improvements. I also see several extra items on the new desk, and a bigger so-called mini bar for the food and wine; we emptied it last time with our after-party gathering, and all the extras, I recall. That was a good farewell night, Giorgio! The function hall was just big enough, and the quantities of food and drink, it has always amazed me just how much champagne the ladies can drink and where they put all the food."

"Emilio, thank Lucia for me, for remembering to stock up on all the extras and office equipment we need; although looking at some of the extra equipment this large suite has, which I normally enjoy, I know these will be for meetings only."

"Very true Giorgio! We can have the first unofficial meeting now at the new desk with the complimentary coffee and excellent selection of sandwiches. And the first item on the agenda: a sealed message from central for you, which arrived as I was leaving to pick you up."

"The familiar envelope, eh, Emilio."

"Some things never change, Giorgio, and sometimes it's good news."

"This one is. It's a confirmation of a message I received from D section yesterday. It must be the same as you received, and it's more or less what we discussed on our way here, my eight days in Athens are cancelled and so on and Emilio to liaise, internal department alert, timetable upgrade leave for Cannes office of foreign trade on completion of meetings in Athens. Here, take a look, just to make sure. Oh, and pass it on to Lucia for me; you know how she likes to file all our reports, no matter how minor."

"It is the same, Giorgio, and that's why I am still here. As you saw in my report, all this is due to unauthorised removal of documents. Vital information to the Athens independent finance meetings were taken from their offices of social learning."

"It's an interesting title, eh Emilio, for a so-called security department. I wonder about the people who make these decisions and apply quirky names. They must be rotated ex-employees from ad agencies."

"Giorgio, nothing surprises me with that organisation; it's a place of no organisation. How did it go on your possibly last tour of the Middle East? Anyone or anything I should know about that is not in the report?"

"I have a couple of names and contacts for you to check, otherwise, no major problems worth noting. It all went surprisingly well. Almost everyone expected the reorganising and upgrading of company procedures. Streamlining will make the next full round trip of all our Middle East businesses much easier. Those unaware or not informed of our new system were happy to leave for the home office, albeit with immediate effect, apart from that it was all very low-key and straightforward. I did leave a few days early, missing out on a small farewell day, which would have been a dry affair, and a couple of days briefing others on all the updates, which will now fall on to a couple of our younger colleagues, who I'm sure will be happy to gain the experience of it all."

"I know both, Giorgio. They will cope all right, especially after they receive my instructions."

"Nice touch, Emilio! Anyway, I was to return to Monaco via Cannes, and of course, that was changed to Athens, and that's it. You know the details of my new assignment, to adjust my travel arrangements to reflect ongoing changes in this sector, proceed from Athens to Cannes office via Rome at your discretion. It was eight days in Athens for departmental meetings, and now it's only four days. All with immediate effect. So, as time is pressing, Emilio, what's the business itinerary you have for me?"

"You're right, time is pressing, Giorgio. We only have four days and three nights here in Athens to assess what is going on and flush out as much as possible. Who is behind it all and their motive? We have two meetings lined up: a business one tonight and a buffet evening tomorrow. I don't have all the details for that yet. And the last night is a more upmarket business meeting. Tonight, it's a low-profile gathering of business and finance groups, general introductions and low-key chitchat, with cold buffet sandwiches and good vintage wine. It's an ideal opportunity for you to meet the group chairman, but mainly, Antonio and his sister. I shall call for you at 18:00. You have 3 hours to be ready, and no time for sightseeing or personal socialising, eh, Giorgio."

"I know you have my interest at heart, Emilio," Giorgio said smiling. "I read your priority report as to Antonio's recent background; it would make a good story. However, I have a feeling there's more."

Chapter 2

First Meeting

"This is good Emilio—an impressive first night turnout. Everyone's socialising and enjoying the evening with a lot of enthusiasm between the groups. I've been listening closely and reading between the lines. There are some big financial incentives flying about. Have you heard anything, Emilio?" "Only as you've heard, but it is something to do with the Wednesday meeting. It's still early yet. As the evening progresses and more refreshment has been consumed, it will loosen a few more tongues."

"Bearing that in mind, Emilio, I think it's time for a coffee and another sandwich from the catering bar. They also have a fine selection of desserts. As my first social business meeting for a month, this is turning out to be a very good evening, as you know I enjoy meeting new faces. You're enjoying the wine. The food is excellent. I'm now looking forward to the whole evening, seated here as we are between the food and the bar—an excellent position to observe."

"I agree with that, Giorgio. It is a good vantage point."

"Well, Emilio, we've met several of the financial staff, mixed with a few of the high rollers. Maybe, it's time for you to introduce me to a few of the more interesting people on our list, as they are all now relaxed and settled into the evening."

"Ok, Giorgio. We should start with one of our main interests, the finance chairman who looks slightly bored now."

"Ok, Emilio. After that, we should be ready to ask the right questions to the very interesting couple over by the bar."

"Of course, Giorgio. I suppose it's nothing to do with his sister, and I'm not going to tell you her name; she can introduce herself."

"Why not? You big bastard! She's not dangerous, is she?"

"Yes, she can be indirectly."

"Ok Emilio, point taken. I shall bear it in mind when we're talking. Let's go meet the chairman, and before we do, who's the charming woman whispering in his ear?"

"That is Eva, the chairman's secretary. A formidable lady as you can see. It's in her eyes. What do you say, Giorgio?"

"Well, she's almost handsome, apart from her being able to outstare an owl. Is there anything else I should know about her? Anything on file?"

"No, she is well-liked, and has her ear to the ground as you say, but we have no file or details."

"Ok, let's say hello and see if we can make them smile with a few indiscreet comments."

***

"That was an almost interesting waste of time. What did you think of the chairman and Eva, Giorgio? As it's your first time meeting both, you may see something else."

"Eva was very quiet but very sharp. I suspect she keeps tab on everything discussed, pointing out who's who. Not sure, what category we came under? I also think she would protect him physically; she has that certain something, a ruthless streak about her. Mind you, she would need it, as he's a bit chinless. As for the chairman, he's one of the world's great talkers; although he did make several valid points about foreign business and its financing, in particular the trust shown in some financiers putting big money upfront for some big deals to be discussed on Wednesday. I had a feeling that he wasn't supposed to talk about it. Did you see Eva give him those sideways looks? I wouldn't like to have been on the end of one of those. And the land deals with whatever else he and his colleagues are handling, as big as the finances are that go with it, could easily turn someone with ambition and big ideas, like Antonio."

"I am glad it is not my line of business, Giorgio, unless it involves increasing our section and expenses. But I saw the looks from Eva, who is good at her job to see and understand what he should say, and how to keep him in line when he is talking is different."

"That's an interesting point, Emilio. I wonder how much power she has. I would like to know how they payroll his department and expenses. They certainly spend plenty organising these not-so-little gatherings, and moving money around. Any ideas, Emilio?"

"Probably better not to know, Giorgio. Those people are like grey shadows in the dark; we are probably the only ones who see them. Well, I have a hunch that meeting Antonio may answer a few of our questions, and bring us in to the light. I saw him look our way a couple of times when Eva was speaking to you."

"Come on, Emilio, no time like the present. Let's go over and have a chat before they move from the bar."

"Good evening, Antonio, Francesca. I would like you meet my colleague and friend Giorgio."

"Good evening, Giorgio." They said simultaneously. Antonio pushed his hand forward in front of Francesca and gripped Giorgio's hand firmly with a cold look.

✳✳✳

"Well, Giorgio, now that they've departed, I think that drink would be in order."

"We're at the bar, Emilio. What are you having?

"A large wine as that Antonio wasn't in the mood to drink with us, especially after some of your getting-to-the-point comments. It might have been a bit too much for him, although his sister found them interesting, trying to hold back a smile a couple of times."

"That's true, Emilio. Anyway, tell me what you were thinking. I could see that coded look you use."

"Giorgio, we will have to be careful; he is tolerating us for how long, who knows. You're right. I've seen that cold empty look before. I would say that he and Eva have a lot in common, both very calculating. Well, we both have a clearer understanding of Antonio's goals in the financial sector, and nothing's going to stand in his way, not even us. Giorgio, he would be a hard man to bring down. I agree and, in more ways than one, his sister was far more cautious. I got the feeling that she could have kicked him a couple of times for excess talking and treating her as if she was just some junior employee. It's very odd behaviour for a brother. But he certainly can talk, fortunately for us. He and the chairman must be very close, as one of them is schooling the other. They're both spouting the same bullshit phrases, and it's very hard to believe Antonio's role with the office of social learning. What is in it for him? There's something that doesn't make sense. It appeared to be more his sister's role. But I do believe his meteoric climb in the business world and his success over the last four years is incredible.

"Emilio, we're missing something. Can you get me his life story? Something for me to read on the ferry to Brindisi. All I know is, he's 40 and Italian, if that's true."

"You may have to wait until Brindisi. We have been watching his coming and going for some time, but they are only local details. Everything else will have to come from central."

"Does he have any other contacts in this office, Emilio? Yes, one or two low-key personnel and one particular unpleasant character called Ponte, a real heavy weight, usually armed. He is strongly linked to various corporate finance people as a go-between. He's in the file."

"Is there anything on file about Antonio's sister, or should I say Francesca?"

"Her main area is Italy, with occasional visits to Athens and Monaco. She's a high-profile advisor administrator, who is well-connected, especially in Rome. Be careful with her, Giorgio. She has influence and friends who would do her serious favours because of her family connections."

"I will thank you. It would account for her reaction when I mentioned that I was here as an industrial coordinator. I looked directly into her eyes; I could almost see her mind running through files about us. 'Really,' she said in a matter-of-fact way. That was more or less what I said to her when she told me she was here as a language translator."

"All women just think too much. And we know why, Giorgio?"

"Tell me again, Emilio."

"Well, I blame the corpus callosum. It's got a lot to answer. For girls have the best of it, maybe. It's a good job they don't know it's medical and it's online. The connection between the left and right side of the brain is called the corpus callosum. During the day, it transfers information of about 70% in women and about 50% in men, and at night, 7% in women and in men it drops to 1%."

"So, Emilio, they never stop thinking. It must be very difficult to concentrate on particular items because they can't stop thinking of everything, and it makes sense why women are always talking to each other."

"You're right, Giorgio, and as you know, I have had two wives, maybe one or two other ladies, one of whom was a physician who gave us both this information some time ago, so we have learned much and what to look out for."

"You're right, Emilio. I remember the physician in question. It's good to know, and best not to think too much about it."

"Well said, Giorgio!"

"Thank you, and which brings us back to Antonio's sister. Emilio, can you check both of them? Go back as far as you can; I know you're going to look back on Antonio, but I think it might be worth paying to look even deeper. There's something about Antonio."

"I will check. Leave it with me. Let's go through to the lounge area, Giorgio. We can sort out tomorrow's itinerary."

"And you my friend can check if your aide, or to give Lucia her correct title, your executive PA, has called in."

"You heard, then, Giorgio. Just a little iron man, she's just a slip of a girl, but she could be worse than a force ten gale if you don't keep her up to date, with all our sea experience. We both know it's like a ship at sea; you have to ride it out or find a safe haven. And here we are in the calm alcoholic waters of the small lounge bar. Sadly, you're right, Giorgio."

"So, the lovely Lucia told you off for not telling her about the office reorganisation or her promotion, probably a little understandable, although it was only a minor slip. How did she find out?"

"If only I knew, I should have told her sooner."

"Never mind, Emilio. She's just toying with you because she likes you. She's probably known for some time, that's what Lucia does. She knows what's going on, and even worse, she practically knows everything, reading our reports, knowing our movements,

Cheer yourself up, Emilio! There's always some poor bastard feeling worse. Read this. You'll feel better. It's my latest update report, which should bring a smile to your face. We're all in it. Even though, I've only just arrived with nothing real to go on, it was fairly straightforward to write, but we sound so professional, which I think we are, and all ready to go come what may. Whether they believe it at the top, is another matter."

"Talking of the top, Giorgio, an item came down the vine that could involve you. There's a lot of unusual activity and people about all linked to the meetings that are taking place, so I have arranged safe transport for you during your stay."

"Armed security this is not like the department trying to keep me upright, it's usually the reverse. Do they know something, Emilio?"

"It's just a precaution. You know your new escort—she's from D section."

"Tactical Elana, eh? Well that's put a stop to my days out for a good lunch with our colleagues, you're included in this Emilio. She'll be watching the clock for us, and I shall have to be good now if I want to keep my goodish name intact. There's always a catch. I suppose Elana will be in the lower car park."

"The car is, Giorgio. Your escort is now Angelina who will be in the D section area, probably, having coffee with the secretaries talking about how you left last time."

"Ah Angelina. Yes, it was your promotion celebration at the hotel, that was a good twenty-four hours—one of our better parties."

"It was Giorgio! You and Angelina had a good night up to a point."

"Yes, we did, and I know what you're referring to as well. The trouble with Angie is, she's very sharp, one of those women who might remember unnecessary small details."

"I think hiding her best glittery party shoes, so she couldn't start her exotic dance for us all wasn't a small detail. We were disappointed, but Angie was just a touch annoyed at the time, even though it was wine-induced. It will take more than chocolates this time, Giorgio."

"I'll try to think of something, not that it will do much good."

"So, tell me Emilio, before I venture down to D section, have we made progress, putting all our knowhow to the test on everyone we've met? And is this going to be the pattern for the Wednesday meeting?"

✳✳✳

"Giorgio, we have made a good entrance and progress. Everyone is now aware of our presence, and most importantly, we have more than made Antonio aware of us, which is good. It adds to their pressure. I wonder if they will show up on Wednesday. As for the night itself, I'm sure it will be more or less the same as tonight, with one slight variation, there will be an opening guest speaker, with the main theme being foreign business, oil, gas and land deals.

We will be guests of the finance minister this time. We only need to observe, having met the main players already, so just generally blend in meet those who we feel are people of interest to us, and see if we know any of the new associates, as I am told there will be an extra twenty to thirty guests, food and drink very much the same so there is an upside. I shall pass on the who's who list to you in the morning, Giorgio. I'll take it that you will be around tomorrow afternoon."

"I shall be in the office, Emilio, and you've forgotten about the department. Haven't you? Mind you, after the last one, which you somehow missed, turned in to a hell of a mess. Some of the girls were very upset, not knowing if they were invited or not. There were a whole lot of apologies the next day, and it wasn't good. So, this time it's for "all" department personnel, commencing midday with a one-hour buffet lunch, followed up with an evening meal, music and "the whole works;" it all kicks off from 18:00. It's a thank you to everyone from the upper powers and me, for all their efforts in keeping me mobile and updated with everything. It's been on the books for almost a year, and no one in the whole section has forgotten.

And just to make sure of this fact, the ladies in D section, who source my messages, sent me a gentle reminder, I quote: 'Giorgio, we look forward to your presence. We are all ok at this end. Looking forward to the great night. Bring your wallet, especially Emilio.' All on confirmation message paper signed the office, stuck on top of your priority messages and sent to the Middle East section for my attention, which I received about a week ago."

"It's difficult to hide anything from those girls, I know, especially if one is now your escort driver."

"They are a good team Emilio, with a great sense of humour, but they all need a good break from the roller-coaster workload, especially with the messages that pass through their hands."

"Giorgio, I shall mention that to Lucia about the D section and the workload. I think she would like to do something for the section, having seen a recent report from central that could increase the pressure."

"You're now a section head and soon-to-be-commander, Emilio. You have the authority to request a review."

"Me a commander, Giorgio? It's hard to imagine the position when I'm just sitting at a desk going through reports, writing reports, people coming and going, calls messages. Fortunately, Lucia deals with most of the day-to-day running. It is not the same as when you and I were at sea. We were self-sufficient for our own section. We were almost independent of the commander, with every facility, every day something new to resolve, and visiting new and old places. I have made my speech, Giorgio."

"It's best to remember the good times. Now, you're their figurehead, and you will know the tricks that junior staff can get up to, not that they were that old."

"If it makes you feel any better, I have the same feelings remembering those times, but I wouldn't go back. I'm a little more fortunate possibly. I still get to travel. No anchor for me, but the very important. "But," every now and again all of us get to have a break and a bloody good time, and this one is tonight.

It's possibly the last one here, so let yourself go, Emilio. We're all going to have a great night.

And you my friend will definitely be there this time to enjoy it all, as Lucia will make sure you don't try to sneak off on some so-called dangerous secret jaunt somewhere. She is now fully in charge of your days, as you will see from the new itinerary on your desk, courtesy of Lucia, your now executive PA, who will be accompanying you. She also thanks you for her official executive guest invite, telling me that you were very thoughtful to remember as you were always so busy and under pressure.

So, two things, Emilio. You organised Lucia's invite and that both of us need to remember the official title. We need some sort of signal. Scratch your ear or something. Neither of us want to get it wrong after all the recent events."

"Giorgio, I shall be asking you to keep a good weather eye on what I say, especially half way in to the evening."

"Ok, I get your drift. Although with Lucia by your side all evening, I don't think you're going see too much vintage wine, especially large."

"Why do you think that Giorgio?"

"You may have the title, Emilio, but as the good PA that she is, she will be advising you and looking after your health. Reflecting back, Lucia has always looked after your interests. Have you ever noticed, Emilio?"

"She just always seems to be there, Giorgio, doing a good job for the company and me."

"A word of advice, Emilio. I wouldn't say that to her if I were you, and again that also goes for the title and especially the invite, as I organised it along with a few others while I was in D section."

"I won't Giorgio, and a small detail for you, when you have the chance check your messages at D section."

"I can't avoid it, with my shadow from D section knocking me up early and probably waving her glittery shoes at me. That's knocking on the door, Emilio, not the American expression."

"I understand, Giorgio. You having one of the ladies from D section; it would not work."

"I wouldn't put it exactly like that, but yes, and there's an upside to all our pressures. It's a free night tomorrow for all; no wallet required. The powers at central have agreed to our request, and it's a small price to pay to rebuild all the lost goodwill through penny-pinching last time. And Lucia has organised your favourite wine, she sees something in you."

"What can I say? Thank you, Giorgio, Yes is all I can say. Good. See you tomorrow mid-morning."

✳✳✳

Giorgio rang down to the reception.

"Hello Giorgio. Would you like me to put you through to Angie?"

"No, just tell her, I'm on my way down. I'll meet her at the car."

"I shall, Giorgio. Have a good evening.

"Thank you, Maria."

"Giorgio," Angie said sharply. "You are not supposed to be here alone."

"There are so many people about from the meeting. I should meet you at the reception office. I thought it would be safe enough walking down on my own."

"Get in the car, Giorgio. I shall take you to your hotel."

Giorgio sat quietly as Angie navigated her way out of the safe area of the complex and in to the busy night traffic; it was only a twenty-minute drive from the outskirts in to the bright city lights.

Angie glanced at Giorgio a couple of times; two minutes later, she broke her silence.

"You're looking very well, Giorgio. How is everything?"

"I'm well, and you're looking extremely well, Angie. I see you have the attaché case. Is that for tomorrow or Wednesday?"

"For both, most are for immediate attention, so under the circumstances I shall stay to brief you, then I must get back. I shall pick you up at 8:30."

Angie turned in to the hotel staff car park and into a secure guest parking area that came with the suite. They made their way to the lift area, taking the middle lift to the top floor suite. Angie opened the door; putting the lights on, Giorgio followed her in making my way to a big table by the main windows and balcony. Giorgio turned, looking at Angie.

"Ok Angie, I want to apologise for the shoes and."

"What shoes Giorgio? The glittery ones. I have no idea of what you are talking about. When I was here last it was."

Angie laughed.

"All right, Giorgio. You've grovelled enough. I just wanted to hear your excuse. You pain in the arse Angie, had you forgotten?"

"Of course not, but the next day, I felt terrible and sorry. I was glad you took the shoes. It could have been an embarrassing time for me the next day, and you were not here for me to tell you. And I did so want to tell you before you left. I have waited all this time."

"It was only a short time ago."

"It was seventeen weeks ago Giorgio. You have no concept of personal time. After this assignment, I shall be keeping you in closer proximity."

"I like that phrase, Angie."

He took her hand, kissing her on the cheek. Angie sighed, "Giorgio, I could crown you. Come here." She let go of his hand and put her arms round him.

✳✳✳

"I have to go, Giorgio. It's late. I have to pick up a difficult pain in the backside early, who will be expecting his breakfast in bed." "You could stay, Angie." "Giorgio, I cannot. There are always things to do before I see you, and you mister, amongst other things to do, have several low-priority messages, which you must catch up on by mid-morning without fail." "Are you listening?" "Always Angie." "You're hopeless, Giorgio. I shall see you after you have had breakfast."

"Goodnight, Angie. I missed you."

Angie looked at Giorgio as she put her jacket on. "I shall tell you what I think later when my head is clear. Don't stay up late. We have things to do in the morning. Sleep well." As Angie left, Giorgio put a hotel dressing gown over his shorts and walked out of the bedroom to the balcony, where he stood leaning on the wooden topped stone-clad balcony. He could do with a balcony like this in his house, he thought, as he looked out across the rooftops spires and office blocks and listened to the sounds of the city. His mind started to race over all the details of the first night's business meeting and their progress. Emilio needs to call a meeting. They all need to get their heads together. Giorgio certainly had one or two ideas.

✳✳✳

Angie stood talking with Maria at the inner reception office, tailing off a conversation. "I like the name Arabian dancers; it sounds right, Maria." "'Seven Veils' may be misinterpreted." "I agree, Angie, knowing some of the men from the middle office." "Maria, can you tell the others? I shall see you all later; also let Giorgio know, I'm on my way. Tell him to be ready, with emphasis on the ready." "I will Angie," she said smiling.

"Good morning, Angie." "Good morning to you, Giorgio." "Are you lunching in today?" "Sadly not, I'm meeting with Emilio first, and you're taking us to a meeting somewhere in the city. I see in your eyes that you're itching to tell me because I haven't read my updates fully. Then, after that, you will be with me attending an ordnance meeting, which will take us through to mid-afternoon. I have another meeting with central regarding finances and the forthcoming journey to Rome. Go on, Angie, hit me with it." "Where is it? Giorgio, I ought to hit you. You have not read any of the messages. Here's the message. Read it. I thought it was there. They should have come here for the meeting. We have a better canteen on the second floor than they have in the whole place. Giorgio, I do not know what to say to you sometimes because Emilio had forgotten as well, Lucia told me." "Well, there you go then, it wasn't important. Come on, Angie. We don't want to waste any more time on minor issues, Emilio, and I know you always have everything in hand, so let's go."

"Thank you for lunch, Giorgio. I have always liked this little restaurant." "I know, Angie. I thought it would be a good place for us to catch up on a few things, especially after playing you up this morning, and I wanted us to be together before we set off for Patras tomorrow." "You're forgiven this time, Giorgio, and I am so looking forward to this evening. And, there is a little surprise for you—a new costume, and after tonight, I'm sure there will be lots of stories and rumours going around." "Why? Do you know something, Angie? If we had a bit more time." "But we haven't, Giorgio, I have to get you back for your meeting. I will see you at your hotel at 17:20."

✳✳✳

"Hi Angie. I like your disguise—a six-foot trench coat and hat. It just fits your five-foot two skinny frame." "Hey, you know I'm not that skinny. I had to borrow the coat and big hat from one of the security boys. I couldn't change here; it would have taken too long. I brought over a change of clothes for later. I don't want to wear my costume back to my place. You don't mind, do you? It's just so much easier to change here at the hotel."

"Of course not, there are two bedrooms anyway. It's perfect because I need to discuss business with you, an idea I have regarding colleagues of the finance minister. We can talk now and later, if time permits." "It must be heavy duty if you want to discuss it tonight, Giorgio." "It is, and I don't have a lot of time to implement it." "Just a minute, Giorgio. You haven't asked about my costume; just tell me what you think."

Angie took off the trench coat and hat. My mind paused as I took in this vision in what was possibly a costume.

"Angie, you look amazing. The style and the material fit your beautifully shaped figure, and in particular, your shapely naughty bottom so well. I apologise for my skinny remark; it was just a silly." "Stop there, Giorgio. I know what you meant. Remember, I know you very well, and what you're saying. And thank you, Giorgio, for your kind observation. Anyway, just briefly, seven of us are going to be the Arabian dancers. We will make it clear from the start. We will not be removing any veils. Maria and I talked it over."

"That's good to hear, otherwise, it could start a riot. This material feels quite flimsy." "Oh Giorgio." "I like the long dark hair as well." "That's my hair, Giorgio. Well, just a few extensions." "There's something about you, Angie; you've changed. You look very different. Oh Angie, put your coat back on. I've almost lost track of everything. What time do we have to be there?" "Elana will be back in twenty-five minutes." "Ok good, Angie, can you sit down all right in the costume?

Yes, why? Take a seat at the table; after last night's business meeting, Emilio and I talking to Eva Antonio his sister Francesca has left me with a dark impression of all of them. I want you to check on the three of them. I shall talk with Emilio tomorrow, but in the meantime, you could make a start by calling central from here. There's also a go-between Ponte, who I should like to meet."

"Yes, I've heard of him Giorgio," as she rang central. "He is someone others try to avoid."

"Hello Jody, it's Angelina." "Giorgio, I am through to central? Is there anything other than that we have spoken of?" "Not for now." "Giorgio, central are arranging to expedite everything you have requested; I have listed it as a priority through Emilio's section." "Thank you, Jody," and put the phone down. "Nice one, Angie. I shall hint at it to Emilio later and give him the full details tomorrow."

"Have you ever met Francesca?" "Yes, I was introduced at a social meeting in Rome a while back now; I've listened to her at several functions, always on company business when I have accompanied one or more of our committee members. I have also heard unusually interesting rumours about the lady, and to quote a certain person saying, her movements would make your socks go up and down like roller blinds." "Yes, thank you, Angie. It sounds like one of Emilio's sayings." "Yes, Giorgio, it is."

"Sorry Angie. It's time or the shortage of it. I know it's a lot to ask, but please give all these details as much thought as you can allow as it's vital that we organise a plan here at this office, so it's up and running when we are on route. These people are all part of something that is finance-orientated, and somehow it's linked with the offices of social learning and the missing documents, but it's mainly Francesca. She is or was the only person with clearance to the offices. I need the information as soon as you can provide; I also want your personal opinion of her."

"I shall get everyone on to it first thing, Giorgio. Although we have their details on file, it's just general information; you want us to go deep." "Everything you can. I want to know every detail you can lay your hands on, buy it if you have to, especially for Antonio."

"Elana is here. We should go Giorgio. Take the advice you gave Emilio: enjoy the night, and let yourself go." "Thanks Angie. Good advice. I will, and I'll be rooting for you." "We can dance afterwards Giorgio."

✳✳✳

"You made it Giorgio." "Just a little delay on committee business, which I need to discuss with you Emilio. You're looking very lovely in that outfit, Lucia."

"Thank you, Giorgio. You and Emilio look very smart." Lucia stepped closer to me. "Giorgio, I couldn't help but notice on your entrance, who was the lovely lady who rushed off to the cloakroom." "I'm going to keep you guessing for a while as we're on that line of thought. How are you and Emilio in that big new office?" "Well, I shall tell you, Giorgio. He is very difficult to work with; he hardly ever does as I tell him." "I know the feeling, Lucia." At this, Emilio almost gave a loud laugh, but Lucia was present. "And you, Giorgio, can tell us who the girl in the trench coat is. Is she a new detective?" Ah, Lucia started to say something. "Yes, Lucia you were going to say. It will keep Giorgio," she said, smiling at me. "Come, let us enjoy the night."

"Lucia, would you care for a glass of wine?" "Not for me, Giorgio, but Emilio would like a small glass of his usual vintage, after he has danced with me." "I shall leave the wine on the main table, Lucia." "Thank you Giorgio. Enjoy yourselves. I'm going to mingle with the new sand dancing group, forming over on the other side."

Chapter 3

Last Office Social

"Hello Giorgio. All is well with you on this bright and early morning. Let's go through to the cafeteria. We can discuss our strategy for the day as well as hear the stories of last night. In particular, you with one of the Arabian dancers who I seem to recall even with the disguise, and little else resides in D section. I didn't recognise her at first. It was Lucia something to do with the detectives trench coat, and we could see you with the secretaries and others encouraging the dancers. Lucia said Angelina was dancing for you with her flowing veils."

"And, a very good morning to you, Emilio. What's with all this bright and breezy stuff? Have you and Lucia got engaged? And after last night's performance, kissing and dancing, you'll have to get married and make an honest woman of Lucia. I hear you and Lucia are top billing on the office news this morning, with the sand dancers a close second." "We have lost the top billing, Giorgio; it went to the singing group La Dolce Vita, who carried the good life a bit further by stripping at the end of their performance—all done in the best possible taste and so many people joined in, just down to their shorts. I almost joined in, but Angie wouldn't let me. On reflection, I'm glad. I also thought of it, Giorgio, as in our old sporting day but Lucia took me home, saying I have to remain neutral to maintain my position. Did anything happen after we left?" "No that was the climax. We left soon after you with Elana. She dropped us at the hotel and waited for Angie. As Angie got changed, I told her the virgin desert will never be the same after seeing her dance. She said it would give me something to remember. At least, I managed a few hours' sleep. How about you Emilio?" "I did as well, Giorgio, knowing we all have a full day ahead although last night will be on the minds of most and on par with our agenda."

26

"That's very true, Emilio. I had a good talk with Lucia this morning about the Arabian dancers, as we were going through the expenses. Just to clear up any misunderstandings, I explained how I was just one of the many admirers of the dancers, and that Angie had thought it might remind me of my recent desert experiences, but for some reason, Lucia didn't buy it, because she and Angie are old friends so pretty much whatever you and I do will be known, it's a good network. And that Emilio is a lesson for us to remember: women always notice things."

"True, Giorgio, and they are always trying to find out who is doing what. I suppose we have to acknowledge this, as we exploit it sometimes. It's only to be expected from D section, but the secretaries can be quite challenging when they want information."

"Good point about the secretaries. I'll come back to you about that. Anyway, getting back to Lucia, a bit later, she had to mention her now-famous kiss with you, as several D section girls came in, all making remarks about how good the night was and asking after you, Emilio. I didn't know you were so popular. The upshot is I think Lucia likes you a lot as I think she tried to pass on some of her feelings of your togetherness by telling me, 'It's about time you settled down Giorgio. You have been too long on your own since Laura.' I thought she was going to add as settled as Emilio and I. All I could reply was, if you can stop those sealed company envelopes I might have a chance.

Then, Lucia in her nice way, or dangerous way, wanted to talk about you, just small talk, but I didn't crack and tell her the real you wherever that is now. So, apart from all that Emilio, you're in good spirits, and you've enjoyed all this as well as the last night. Haven't you?"

"It was an evening to be remembered, Giorgio. I can hardly believe how good it was, now if only Lucia would tell us what's going on or let me run the office as I need to."

"Emilio, I'm saying nothing about that, but I won't forget last night everyone made it a night that would long be remembered, although some of the sand dancers seem to have conveniently lost their memory, and without too much prejudice, I thought the Arabian dancers, whoever they were all dancing for were unbelievable. The whole office had such a good time.

One piece that won't go away is Lucia kissing you on the dance floor; they all want to know. Well, the women want to know if it means what it looked like. I mean what the hell does that mean. I saw it; it was just a kiss, wasn't it?

Anyway another piece of interesting news for your ears only, more info has come to light on the missing files from the social learning offices. One of the secretaries is very friendly with one of the internal security guards; we can talk later after I check the details. And to tail off on a more personal note, your Lucia did us proud, looked after us all very successfully; it made her very happy, which played on all of us. She also handed me the who's who list with everything else, which is now in the attaché case."

"You're right, Giorgio. We had an evening to remember. Lucia and I danced several times. She really enjoyed that, as you say she kissed me on the dance floor, this is not like Lucia, others noticed but Lucia waved to them all and they all waved back, Lucia told me that we made the perfect dance couple, I agreed, the whole evening was well received and enjoyed by everyone." "It was Emilio and Lucia is a good woman. I thanked her this morning for all her help in processing and expediting everything while we're on the move, and you're a lucky guy, Emilio." "Thank you, Giorgio. I hope the future is kind to us that we are able to return to this night, but who knows what waits for us out there."

"We need these things to happen, Emilio. It takes the pressure off for a few hours; I would be more than happy to have another night as I had. Hopefully everyone had a good night, as there's little chance of another time."

"I think you're right, Giorgio. We need to make the best of every day for those we care for and those we protect. As for all life, death is certain and life is short. The next few days may prove that maxim for someone, whatever happens it's going to be tense." "Very true words,

Emilio, and tonight's little gathering will be the opening gambit, which you and I will see through whatever they throw at us. See you later in the reception lounge at 19:00; it should give me enough time to check our latest well-obtained info and the who's who list. I might even get time to sort out the finances for the next seven days." "You mean increased expenses, Giorgio."

Chapter 4

Second Meeting

"Well, that was an interesting opening to the last night. Let's take a seat at one of those tables near the bar, Emilio, before the rush. I think we're entitled to a drink after listening to those dry and sombre words. What did you think of the opening speech? What are you having, Emilio?"

"It was OK. 15 minutes is long enough if you're not interested, although going by the cheers everyone else thought it was good. I'll have a large wine. Something for your interest, Giorgio, have you seen who is with the deputy finance minister, our friends Francesca and Eva and no Antonio, very interesting do you not think?"

"I am a little surprised but I've seen the reason why they left a very slippery character behind to keep an eye on things. Behind the minister, the one with the goat beard that looks like a rat behind a toilet brush, do you recognise him?"

"Yes, an old acquaintance, Giorgio, from three years ago about artwork in Florence. That sounds about right for him, but why would Ponte be using a low life document forger like Tullio. You don't like him do you, Giorgio?"

"You're right. He is definitely trouble; whenever he turns up, so do bodies, no doubt this time courtesy of Ponti or possibly Antonio. If he's here, someone has or is about to lose something. He's talking and trying it on with Eva. I would love to know what it's about. Eva's trying to stand slightly back; I don't think she likes skinny runts like Tullio either."

"What you're saying, Giorgio, is that he is not trustworthy even amongst his own."

"That's definitely what I mean you should watch out for him, Emilio. He is the classic betrayer, especially where big payoffs are made. You remember the motor yacht that sank, leaving Malta, and nothing of value was found on board?"

"I remember, Giorgio. It was never resolved. The loss of artwork and government documents, all presumed lost at sea. He was somehow linked to that. The file is still open on the incident and Tullio. It was a serious incident, Giorgio. I think we will both need to be more vigilant."

"We will. I wonder who's watching who now, Emilio, and I wonder why Antonio's not here. I'm just generally suspicious of some of his motives for that matter, Ponte's as well. Are they setting Tullio up or is Tullio setting" "Antonio and Ponte up and what's Eva's position in all this. Giorgio, Eva is leaving with Tullio and the deputy minister. No, they have stopped. Raised voices, this is not good in front of such people; we do not want to be seen to be involved."

"You're right, Emilio. The minister is returning to his group. If we stay here in the bar, I can relay everything I see on this side. If you move your chair round a bit further and watch the minister on the other side to see if he or any others around him act out of character, we can be ready for any involvement."

Giorgio continued: "Eva and Tullio are out in the hallway. Tullio's holding an envelope up to Eva's face. They are both talking. What's happening your side, Emilio?"

"All calm. Francesca is talking to several financiers."

"Things are happening this side. Eva has tried to take the envelope. There's a lot of arm waving from both now. I can see Eva clearly through the glass doors. She's doing most of the talking;. She's slapped Tullio's face; he's pushed her. She's coming back in alone."

"She looks really pissed off. This just gets better and better."

"Where is she Emilio?"

"Eva has stopped by one of the tables. I think she is trying to compose herself straightening her jacket. She is now stood next to Francesca; she's taken hold of Francesca's arm. Giorgio, can you move here to see it is unbelievable behaviour? I hope it turns in to a cat fight. Francesca is trying to pull away. Now, the deputy minister is there talking to both; he's spoiled it. It's a pity you can't see from your position."

"Sorry, I missed it, but I wanted to see if Tullio would come back in, not sure where that corridor leads, Emilio. It would be best if we deliberately avoid all of this for the whole evening. We could not have planned it any better. Tullio's now out of the picture up to no good somewhere. They need some sort of guidance after that little fracas, and with no Antonio or Ponte to pass information on to it, leaves them exposed and frustrated. With us keeping clear, I'm sure it will arouse curiosity as to why and maybe or hopefully cause more irritation."

"Things are happening for us, Giorgio. When Antonio finds out what has happened, he will be very displeased with Tullio. I am wondering whether Tullio has an ulterior motive for goading Antonio."

"Come on, Emilio. I think we should have another glass of wine and talk to the secretaries. They hear all the gossip, and with what has just gone down, this is major gossip on the doorstep."

"They know many secrets, Giorgio, maybe 75 to 80 percent of all that's going on in and out of the department, and you and I, my friend, are struggling to keep the other 20 to 25 percent from them."

"Emilio, if we survive their interrogating ways tonight we can pool our information at the office tomorrow, and don't forget to buy something for Lucia before we get under way."

"I am glad you reminded me. So much is happening. Lucia is asking me very strange questions since the department do. What I think of gardens? Wouldn't I be better off living in a house than a small apartment? It would be more beneficial for entertaining, especially if it is near Rome. Maybe I should take up sailing again, Giorgio. I could take cover over the horizon from her stretching arms."

"It's just Lucia's way. She likes you. Well, maybe it's time you said to yourself, finish with engines and tie up alongside Lucia. She's a one off, and you need her."

"It's that big step again, Giorgio."

"True, but you're older and wiser, and you hold a responsible position. Lucia is right for you; you know it. When we finish this trip, all will be clear for you both. Anyway when I visit again, I know where to find the best cooked food, as you will both be hosting dinner parties in a large well laid out party garden."

"You put forward a good picture. Maybe, you're right. We can if time permits to talk again on route. Time is escaping, Giorgio. Elana our new driver will be here soon. I must organise my timetable for the train. I have a feeling there's a slight change of plan, possibly the one we discussed. Yes, Lucia has organised the ticket changes. Angelina, will be your business associate and security. I added another change; she has a new piece for you with various clips with the normal add-on items as well as one or two general documents. Your other document requests will be delivered direct to you in one of our standard travel bags by company courier in Brindisi, plus, of course, updates Lucia has organised, and new hardware for both us, which I have organised."

"Ok, Emilio. Sounds good. I have everything secured in the attaché case, mingling slightly inappropriately with a homemade packed lunch courtesy of Lucia, who says I don't eat enough and not at the proper times."

"Hey, you might get away with it, but I'm not brave enough to say any different. Giorgio, it's the same for me. Well, that's good to know, at least there's no wine with it. Right attaché case keys, Lucia has one, she has attached another to your set, and of course, I have one. Time for me to check my tickets to Cannes and collect my documents. I shall see you in Patras."

"Did Lucia sort out Angie's expenses?"

"Yes, all done. Have a good journey, Giorgio. I shall meet up with you both on the station. There is a very good cafe in the main area excellent food and coffee. I shall reserve a table for the three of us. We can go over our notes. You have a good spotter with you. This will be good for her first field work experience to be with you. Now, it begins, Giorgio. We will see who or what may follow us on route. Good luck my friend."

"And a safe journey to you Emilio."

✳✳✳

Giorgio went down to reception. Maria greeted him.

"Hello Giorgio, Angelina is waiting for you."

"Ok Maria. Don't ring through. I want to see what she's up to"

"She will be having coffee and talking as you're late, Giorgio."

"How do you know Maria?"

"One of the secretaries dropped of your tickets to Patras and told me your morning schedule."

"Those secretaries. Does Angie have the tickets?"

"Yes Giorgio." She said smiling. "Have a good journey."

"Thanks Maria."

Giorgio made his way through the file office with a nod from security, before entering the admin offices. He thought to himself: be brave, Giorgio, it's only D section. He looked through one of the windows. It looked, as always, like a hive of activity, a wall of communication machines stretching of in to the distance with other technical bits and pieces all lit up humming away, and there was Angie, cup in hand, talking in the middle of it all. Giorgio entered.

Angie watched him as he walked through. "Coffee Giorgio? She called out with a smile.

One of the girls piped up, "We don't see you in here very often, Giorgio."

"You're right, Donna. I've heard strange stories of certain associates disappearing after stepping in here." Angie came over. "Now Giorgio, it's only because the sensible ones amongst us have taken them off to a safer more fulfilling life." "Well, it sounds good. I hope that's right." "Come on, Giorgio, time for a coffee."

"Here you are, Giorgio, fresh hot coffee compliments of D section."

"Thank you, Gina."

"You're always welcome, Giorgio. We know where you're going next. Take care. Safe journey from all of us."

"Rosa, where are the homemade biscuits."

"By the armoury door."

"There your favourites, Giorgio. Garibaldi's."

"Thank you, Caprice. How did you know that?"

"You always eat them when you're here, which is rarely, and Angelina told us." Several of the girls started calling out to Giorgio.

'Giorgio, when is Emilio going to marry Lucia?'

'What's he afraid of?'

'Tell him, we all want an invite.'

'What about you, Giorgio. You're available.'

'No, he's not.'

"Now girls" Angie called out. "We haven't got time for lots of questions here. I will let you all know when I get back." A small cheer went up from two or three on the far side. "Come on, Giorgio. We should leave. I don't want you disappearing since I'm responsible for you. You weren't very responsible in the. Giorgio, we have to go there listening. Course there not. "Not very responsible in the what, Angie." "You were saying, Giorgio" "Come on. Elana is bringing the car to the front. We have a tight schedule to keep." "Goodbye ladies. Enjoy yourselves." "Bye Giorgio. Look after Angie and yourself."

Angie and Giorgio left for the hotel. Giorgio packed as Angie did her usual nosy act. "I'll help in a moment, Giorgio. Just let me finish here." "I know what you're doing, Angie."

"What's that then, Giorgio." She said sitting up straight. "You're sitting, emptying the correspondence bag in to my attaché case, reading all the reports and the now not-so-personal documents as they pass in front of you, again I might add." "Sorry Giorgio, force of habit, even though it's boring this time. We just like to know everything that's going on, and you always seem to be up to something. On the serious side, every scrap of information helps us to keep you all safe."

"An interesting point of view but Emilio and I know you girls including the secretaries who can be extremely unscrupulous; they are always trying to find out information that we are trying to keep from you." Angie laughed. Reaching out, she took Giorgio's hand. "You men. You are definitely in the right business. You and Emilio are right, of course. We shouldn't know everything. It makes us vulnerable. It does help sometimes, and you Giorgio, you're always trying to get information or something from us or me, and sometimes you do."

"Angelina." "Yes Giorgio," folding her arms across her stomach, "Did I say something? You only use my full name when I do." "Angie, we have a train to catch. There's packing to finish. Elana will be back to collect us in approximately forty-five minutes. I want to discuss some ideas I have, of those involved. You may come up with a different angle on the situation." "All right. Go on, hit me with it as you say. I can see we're not going to have a quiet five minutes together while we can."

"Angie I would like five minutes to get information from you, as you say, but I need to get these ideas clear in my head and your thoughts as well before we board the train, so let's go through everything and take it from there. And as my new business associate, you have some equipment for me, where do you have it hidden." "Giorgio, I could so easily alter that equipment phrase, but as your new associate temporary protector, I shall revert to my hard clear-headed way, well when we leave for the station. In the meantime, you could search me, but it's in the car with Elana." "Angie your such a." "Yes, Giorgio. I am, and as your new associate responsible for your safety as well, I'm in charge."

"Do you have the tickets, Angie?"

"I do, Giorgio." Brushing a few bits of his jacket with her hand.

"Do I have anything on me?"

"No, you look good Angie, as always."

"Why did they choose the train, Giorgio?"

"The train was preferred in the original assignment details from Emilio and central, as several ministry people and others find it more convenient for discussing ideas, and generally just to relax. There are possibly other reasons for some.

Emilio and I will use it to our advantage to gather more information, like who is travelling with who, and generally, keep a high profile on those we feel could help us, or it could unnerve someone in to making a mistake. We've already rattled a few associates at the two meetings. Many who attended the Athens meetings will be at the delegate's diner on the ferry. This is a crucial meeting for us, as private and ministerial finance will be attending. It's going to be very high profile, so whoever is behind this elaborate affair will have to have everything sown up by tonight. When the ferry docks tomorrow, they'll all be going their separate ways.

With you and I going to Patras, I did think we could split the train up between us but as Emilio has left on the earlier train, others may assume I would be on the same train. So, I will stay in the compartment out of the way. You can start at the back walk through to the front, then make your way back to the compartment and give me a run down if no one of interest is on board. We can lunch in the buffet car and make a few notes. Angie, you know the itinerary?"

"Yes, I stay with you at the station in Patras until we meet up with Emilio. I return to Athens on the same train we arrived on. Before that, we all compare notes who was on his train who was on our train. I have fifty-five minutes to have coffee and make my notes if you think it's necessary. You and Emilio go on to Brindisi, meet with the company courier, exchange bags if there is anything to return for us or central, from there travel by train to Rome."

"That's it, Angie. Oh that reminds me."

"What Giorgio?"

"The hotel couldn't obtain tickets from Brindisi to Rome with sleeping compartment at such a short notice; we have to check availability when we arrive at the station."

"You could ask at the station here to check and reserve a compartment if any cancellations come up." "Ok Angie. Good idea."

"Before you continue to Cannes, Giorgio, this case has to be resolved. Is there a deadline for Cannes or a contingency plan?"

"No Angie, and I have no sensible answer for you. My head is filled with everything bar that. There's no plan B; we make this work in the time we have. That's why Emilio and I are pushing things to make it happen. It's a risky strategy, certainly not textbook as you may see it, but there are disagreements within the group, we shall exploit them with Francesca's help."

"With Francesca's help? I would like to know how Giorgio. You obviously have a…, well I don't know. I wish I were going with you Giorgio as your protector or maybe I should use the term security; it would be another pair of eyes and ears. It's important to achieve live-field experience; I also see the disadvantages as well, especially now you have told me how you intend to take advantage."

"I would say to take the initiative, Angie."

"Yes, I would too if I had thought of it. It is a risky strategy, but it's direct."

"Thank you, Angie. Emilio and I need you here. You know how we work, that's everything to us, and we rely on your department to follow up on those names and accounts we worked on and all the other changes. When we resolve this assignment, which we will, my original trip to Cannes will continue, with a few changes here and there."

"Giorgio, we that is D section. Hope you and Emilio have an uneventful journey, although from all the recent events, signals and signs to date, something is just waiting to happen, but when and where we don't know."

"As I said Angie, we need you here to put into place these changes plus anything we think of on route, I'm sure something will crop up; you'll be there as it happens no need for me to spend time making a report for you and the department."

"Giorgio, you must be careful. I won't talk to you if anything happens."

"If it's that bad Angie, I won't hear the silence."

"Giorgio, I hate you not taking it seriously."

"Then, why are you holding my hands?"

She stared into Giorgio's face. "To stop me hitting you. Damn you Giorgio, this is not some silly rugby or football game. You should remember we see your messages from here and there. Listen button head the department have an unusual extra payment structure on a round trip basis and I intend to collect what's mine every time and see those with me do the same, you're the one who sees to it that we receive the up-to-date intelligence, so it's you and the department who see us back, so why should I worry? Is that a good enough answer? It's barely to rubbish. I'll take that as an ok then, so if it's all right with you, can we get on and catch our train. 'Yes, and you wait till we get on it.'

Chapter 5

The Audacious Plan

Elana dropped Giorgio and Angie at the station in good time. She organised their bags to be taken to the train and passed over the equipment case to Angie, who gave Giorgio a sideways look. Giorgio straightened up a little, turning to both, he said: "thank you Elana, take care." "You too Giorgio, and you Angie, look after him." They both smiled. Giorgio followed the attendant through a busy station of Friday afternoon. commuters to the train finding our compartment were the attendant placed all the bags.

Giorgio rearranged the bags, placing his attaché case on the small table, pulled the blind on the compartment door, and settled down to read the backlog of his low-priority reports.

Twenty minutes into the journey, Angie knocked on the compartment panel. "Ok Angie, come in." She came in taking off her jacket as she told him what was happening. "Oh Giorgio. I spoke with booking information regarding Brindisi to Rome. They are unable to make the booking."

"Thanks for trying. I shall check at Brindisi. Go on you were saying about walking through."

"I started as we agreed at the far end, walking slowly through the full length of the train, trying to read my tourist guidebook; your key character Tullio is booked in to the second compartment, second coach, from the end. He is with two other men, and they are all seated in the restaurant car, which is half-full. Eva is also seated in the restaurant car with three men—the only one I recognised is the deputy finance minister. I also have their compartment details. I carried on through to the front end. There was no one else. I walked back to here." She said on a high note.

"Well done, Angie. The two of them here has given me an idea for a plan."

"I too have an audacious plan, Giorgio."

"Let's hear yours, Angie. It already sounds better than mine."

"Ok, it's a very straightforward idea, Giorgio. I search Eva's compartment and luggage while they're still in the restaurant car." She paused. "Well Giorgio." "Angie, I think if you feel that confident go for it. Two things: Could the compartment be locked? Second, are they eating or drinking?"

"First, they were holding the menus, ready to order; the other, I have a special set of keys."

"Angie, see you later and order coffees, with everything for us. I couldn't say take care or your too enthusiastic or good for you Angie; I can only think of it and keep my thoughts inside."

"Ok, I just need to change my normal bag for a shoulder bag; I shall order the coffees with pastries on the way through—don't eat them all." "Order a few sandwiches—meat cheese anything." As Angie closed the door, Giorgio reached for the equipment case. After a route round, he decided to load his normal automatic and keep it handy, with another automatic in his belt. He carried on reading, making notes for Emilio and himself on the ferry. The coffee arrived with a variety of sandwiches and pastries; this was a good spread all adding to a positive journey. He started with a pastry just to go with the coffee. The train was crossing the Corinth canal, with no ships, but a very pleasant view. He glanced at the time, noticing he'd eaten most of the sandwiches; time was getting on, a familiar knock followed by Giorgio. He held the automatic under the table. Ok. She came in with her shoulder bag, looking a little heavier and carrying a beach bag as well, looking reasonably calm and fortunately not conspicuous.

Giorgio stayed sitting looking at this unusual sight that was Angie—all she lacked was a striped jumper and black eye mask. "Giorgio," she said looking back out into the corridor she came in closing the door. "Lock it, Angie." "Giorgio," she said again with a hint of excitement in her voice. "I did it just as we said; it all went to plan," she said, putting the extra bag with her shoulder bag down by the table. "Come and sit down, Angie, I'll pour you a coffee. There's obviously no one behind you. Try a sandwich or a pastry. Have a drink of your coffee." "Thank you, Giorgio. It all went so smoothly, but I have a tiny confession to make." Uh, Oh, Giorgio thought she's added something caught up with it all on her first assignment in the field. "Yes, you seem to have a little more than we planned."

"Ok Giorgio. Should I start with Eva's details?"

"You seemed to have seized the opportunity to remove whatever from, let me guess, Eva's and Tullio's."

"Oh, you've spoiled it now."

"Angie, keep back the enthusiasm for now. Let's see what you've got just in case there's a full-scale problem."

"My shoulder bag has items from Eva's, files, letters, a large amount of money in mixed currencies; my beach bag has the same items from Tullio's, except the money looks to be all US dollars in high denomination notes—a very large amount. It all came to me after recalling your report coupled with our talk about Eva and Tullio falling out over something. I have found that something, in brief, if Tullio thinks Eva has taken it with money and Tullio blames Eva. Giorgio, did I do the right thing?"

"When you said audacious, you weren't kidding. To be honest, Angie, anything could happen, but it was a one-off opportunity, you made the right call. We should check and read everything in both bags." Picking up the shoulder bag Giorgio emptied it on the table. "Empty the beach bag, Angie, and count the money while we consider our next move. We should be prepared and try to second guess their move. What would you do if you discovered vital documents and all your pay off cash was missing? Call out the militia, shoot the person that your convinced removed it, or say nothing and wait. Your move, Angie."

"First, thank you Giorgio, for your confidence in me; second, I would wait, look for signs amongst those around that one person. I think now the ferry crossing could be very dangerous, but I don't know."

"That's ok, Angie, neither do I. All we can do is observe and wait. Forget the money, Angie. Let's start reading through the documents. We have less than an hour to sort it all, interestingly, you're here involved in the report for D section. I wonder how the ladies will react."

"In their normal professional way, Giorgio."

"Yes, I can see that. All cheering 'go Angie go,' when we meet up with Emilio and exchange details of your audacious move. He will feel the same. It'll put a big smile on the face of iron man; he likes gutsy moves as I do."

"Why do you call Emilio iron man apart from his size?"

"Way back, in our early days, we used to wager on certain guys being able to bend steel bars; Emilio usually won. It was always a good bonus for us. Of course, he doesn't do it now. We are older, possibly, more responsible."

"Yes, Giorgio, that's of the later part, as you know the girls in D section will be glad of any more little stories you would like to impart, but, from now on, only the little stories. Everything now seems to be stories by report only. I feel I should be saying they're always trying to find out information, which we're trying to keep from you." "Welcome to field work, Angie, as you're a part of this assignment, you can buy the first round for the three of us at Patras." "Giorgio, I cannot afford to. I know that Emilio drinks really expensive wine. I don't have your salaries, so you will both have to drink beer." "That's ok. You can take it out of your bonus."

"I don't receive a bonus, Giorgio." "Course, you do. You put your neck on the line in a big way. Here this is part of it." "A thousand dollar note." "Oh sorry, you can't cash that. Take this pack of fifties." "Giorgio it's," she sat silently holding the money. "Angie, I've just read

Tullio's extortion list. The names on here almost make your hair curl major—top high rollers, industry government and others. The sums involved, it makes my salary look like a gratuity in a good restaurant, of course."

"Are the three of us on the list?" "You might be, Angie, not Emilio and I; we're just too good to be up there, and it's safer on the first rung. "That's not true, Giorgio." "Ok. Do you have the note letter regarding Eva?" "Yes it's, here it is, enjoy." "This is heavy duty. She truly is the Cruella De Vil of this business. She's got the goods on a few people, including Antonio, who has the most interesting family life. Antonio is bleeding the family of cash and property over his illegitimacy and a couple of other items." "Tullio is the same, Giorgio. He has personal details on Eva with inside information on several finance deals." "Angie, all this information is going to take more time than we've got. We need to go over all the details with Emilio. The three of us should be able to unravel it all and come up with a working solution. I don't want to carry it all on to the ferry, and we can use the money to our advantage.

I guess you're wondering about the money, so to save you making a point, I can enlighten you. It's not our money. It's not theirs. It belongs to some miscellaneous fund, and as custodians, we the three of us will use it to whatever end to make this assignment work.

What do think, Angie?" "Giorgio, I like your point of view. It is logical what can I say I'm new." "Well said, Angie. Ask Emilio when we meet up and listen to his logic, it's brilliant." "Well, the train hasn't been stopped, so no one has said anything. We're not far off, maybe ten minutes. Should we wait on the train, Giorgio?"

"Yes, hopefully, you will see everyone pass, then give it another five or six minutes before we make a move. Let's put this money away but keep both amounts of money separate—the small amount in the attaché case and the other cash in my bag. Angie, you need to take five wraps for the payoff and dummy accounts, put it in Eva's bag of cash, not sure yet how much should be in each." "Giorgio, I would put one in each or better still just have one account with ten thousand; it's only a token." "You're right. Let's do that one wrap only. Hang on to the rest, keep it with your wrap in a safe place just in case there's a change of plan. If we need more, we can dip in to the other bag."

"Tullio's bag of cash made Eva's look like small change. I wonder where it came from, Giorgio. Do you think it was a payoff?" "Could be, maybe it will show on the paperwork. I do know all this is down to one girl and her audacious plan. You did it, Angie." "We did it, Giorgio."

"Right, everything else goes into my bag. How are you feeling, Angie?" "I feel in such good form all my time in the department— the messages, the travelling, the meetings. This has been a journey that will never be repeated when I return home tonight. I hope for a good night's sleep, arrive at the office in the morning, sit at my desk thinking as I am now, did I do that?" "You certainly did, Angie. Only you could have, and the sight of you coming into this compartment with those bags is forever etched in my mind." "Giorgio, I shall say goodbye here, while we're alone. Will you hold me for two minutes?"

Chapter 6

Patras

Giorgio and Angie arrived at the port of Patras. The platform soon became very busy. Angie had a good vantage point standing just inside the open carriage door of the first coach. She was able to catch site of Tullio first, with several others followed two minutes later by Eva and the deputy minister surrounded by a small group. She stayed another three minutes before returning to the compartment. "Platform is almost clear now, Giorgio." "Good, we're all packed here. Let's go." They left the train making their way down a now empty platform; it was surprisingly busy round the station area, fortunately not too busy to hide Emilio, who was on the far side watching the platform gate.

"Ok Angie. Let's see if Emilio finds us or we see him first." "I bet you fifty dollars, Giorgio, we see him first." "Hey, now you're talking. I'll take that bet, he sees us first as soon as we leave the platform, for one hundred dollars."

"You're on, Giorgio." They left the platform heading to a cafe on the far side. "You owe me one hundred, Angie. Look behind you." "Emilio, how are you? Where did you come from?"

"Angelina, it's good to see you. I watched you both walking down the platform, as well as seeing our business interests both leaving the station, so we can walk freely." "Well-spotted Emilio! How was it with your journey? Anyone interesting?" "Not a single person but I had a good late morning breakfast in the dining car." "Giorgio, you had an advantage. You know Emilio and how he works." "Now Angie, I don't know him at all. Come on, cough up the one hundred when we're in the cafe."

"Giorgio, you're teaching Angie our bad ways." "I'm not sure about that Emilio." "Giorgio, I'm here and listening. Do you know this café, Giorgio?" "No, Emilio does. He suggested it." "This is a good old place, Angelina. I recommended it to Giorgio before we left that it would be an easy place to meet. It is a classic building with a positive atmosphere, and most importantly, the food is excellent. Good for us to relax before moving on." They entered the cafe into a stylish gallery of artwork and sculptures around the walls with classic tables and comfortable-looking chairs. "I have reserved a table on the far side." "You arranged all this with, Giorgio. Uh o Emilio, I think you may have just lost me the hundred dollars. Giorgio. you are incorrigible." Emilio and Giorgio laughed.

"Angelina, you are very straight up with much to learn." Emilio moved a chair for Angie, and they all sat down. "Thank you, Emilio. Fortunately, I have only forty-eight minutes to discuss this assignment without picking up any extra field customs from you both. This seat is comfy. Are yours the same?" "Now, Angie no trying to change the subject. The first field custom is to order the first round or better buy the bottle, so Angie how about we flick a silver dollar for the thousand-dollar bill against your one hundred." "You're on Giorgio. I shall flick it." "Call Giorgio." "Tails to win." "It's gone on the floor by your shoe Emilio. What is it?" "It is heads. You lose, Giorgio." "I only have this thousand-dollar bill; you wouldn't take that, would you?"

"Yes, I would because you're a rascal," taking it out of Giorgio's hand. "It's the same one you gave me earlier, and it's just found its way home again. I have always wanted to bet with dollar bills as they do in the movies." "Giorgio, your lucky silver dollar." "Give it to Angie to understand things are not always what they seem." "Thank you, Giorgio. I have often seen others with silver dollars, have you Emilio?" "They are just symbols, Angelina. We shouldn't be drawn in by it." "Well, Giorgio. What do you say to that?" "What can I say Angie?" "Not a lot Giorgio. What is the cost of a silver dollar?" "Do you really want to know?" "Yes. Tell me." "I don't know I won it off Emilio." At this, Emilio roared out laughing: "You are both unbelievable." And laughed slapping Giorgio on the arm, "You wait Giorgio; next time, we're on our own somewhere, you're for it. Angie, you are priceless."

"Is it pay off money, Giorgio?" "It looks like it. The sums involved are high and all mainly in US dollars. Eva's bag was mixed currencies, predominantly US dollars in wraps of ten thousand, and Tullio's bag is all US dollars high denomination notes. You just saw one before it disappeared forever."

"Not forever. I shall ask Emilio if he would cash the note so I can buy a round of drinks." "I will cash the note, Angelina, and I will pay for the drinks as you have raised our spirits. Please look through the menu while I talk to the manager." "Angelina, can I see that note. Just checking, Giorgio. We don't want be taken in like a silver dollar." "It's ok." "Thank goodness for that Emilio, otherwise, Angie would be asking for a refund?" "Giorgio." "Yes Angie. Is there anything else I need to do or report? When Emilio returns, we shall go through all the details of the journey, time for you to relax a little and enjoy the food. Emilio can take care of things now." "Thank you, Giorgio," she said softly, squeezing his hand.

"Have you both decided? The waiter will take our orders. You will enjoy this wine, Angelina. It is from their private stock." "Emilio, a toast to our new member of field operations. To Angelina and her audacious plan!" "To Angie!" "This is a rare classic Emilio; I am glad you chose." "Good. So, tell me Angelina. What happened on the train?" Angie relayed everything and how she felt. Giorgio wondered if Emilio could visualise Angie as he did in a mask and stripped sweater. "That is one of the best spur-of-the-moment audacious plans for any one; you will long be remembered for such a move, a very gutsy endeavour Angelina."

"Time is getting on, Emilio. Let's sort out the money for our pay offs and details for Angie to activate in D section." Two waiters brought several large platters of sandwiches, desserts, ice-cream and coffee. All this and only thirty-five minutes to finish it all. "I have a feeling, Giorgio, you and Emilio will do your best." "Sandwich or a cream cake thing, Angie." "Sandwich please, Giorgio, and you and

Emilio shouldn't be eating those big cakes." "I agree, Emilio, no more cakes for you." "I agree, Giorgio, and as a last treat, we should both have that cream nut chocolate torte with ice cream." "Well thought of Emilio, I agree." They cheered quietly and discretely, "would you like the same Angie as a one off?" "You have both done it again—words fail me, and yes, I would love some." "Good for you, Angelina. We are enjoying it all and ourselves on behalf of you; we do not always receive these opportunities." "Emilio, we will need clearance as some of these names in Tullio's list are too high profile to be in any report." "Angelina, will you let central know, we will send details in the normal way. Looks like the others were interested in have flown or drove to Patras earlier using one of the hotels around here to meet." "Looks that way, Giorgio."

They cleared and organised the papers. Emilio sorted the money at a private side table. "Giorgio, I have a figure now for the department with other payments. What's the department amount? Forty-two thousand. The rest are listed. Angelina, this is your bonus balance another fourteen wraps, put it somewhere safe, and don't think about it, without your bold move, well you know." "Giorgio, we can put the finishing touches to this on board. I have organised the bags, and it has been a pleasure Angelina, and safe journey." "Thank you, Emilio. Safe journey to you to," as they shook hands. "Emilio, I'll see you at the top side bar before the delegate's diner." They all left the restaurant. Emilio heading to the dock boarding area, and Angie and Giorgio walked back across the station to the same platform.

"Giorgio, I want to thank you again for all you have said and all you have explained. I understand so much more. I still don't understand how I did what I did." "Angie, you made things happen. We all just go through the motions of one thing or another, come out the other side and don't realise till much later how if then." Angie took Giorgio's hand and said, "I shall think of you, especially when I am using our lucky two-headed silver dollar." She kissed him lightly on the lips, and said "safe journey to you both." She turned stepping up in to the train as the guard's whistle blew.

Giorgio left the ticket office after confirming the ferry departure time, and with no boarding for another two hours, he decided on a coffee, maybe a snack, but definitely no paperwork, and made his way to the aptly named harbour café—a large well patronised establishment. He headed for the unusually long food display counter, studying the huge cake selection available. After two or three minutes of fancying several chocolate type cakes, he decided on something savoury for a change, just to tide him over until dinner. He glanced down the counter catching someone's eye who was also interested in the same counter. He walked over to say hello. She was too quick for him. "Hello Giorgio," she said in a very efficient business manner.

"Francesca, how opportunistic that we should meet here. It gives me the chance to say goodbye as the chance never arose at last night's meeting. Are you seeing someone off?" "No, I am returning to Rome. My work programme in Athens was cut short." "I'm sorry to hear that you have to return, I didn't see Antonio with you at the meeting, I hope he is well." "My brother is fine. He will be joining me on the trip back to Rome."

"That's good. I hope we have the opportunity to all meet up. I'm sure Antonio and I would have a lot to talk about after last night's little commotion. You probably have a lot to catch up on as well. It's something to talk about on the train." "Yes, we will. Thank you, Giorgio." "As you may recall, I too had my stay in Athens cut short, still returning to France this time of the year does have its benefits." "Yes, Giorgio, you mentioned that you were returning to Cannes. Now, we're both here. Do you have good plans for the future and to return to your ship?"

"That's very interesting, Francesca. The ship, the future, as these types of journeys are always a day-by-day thing. Would you care to share a table? We can continue our conversation in private as I am extremely interested in what you thought of last night's meeting and the guest speaker, and, of course, your interests in oil and land deals. As for plans, why should we bother to think of all those boring things? We're here now. Tomorrow and Rome are beyond the horizon." "That's very philosophical, Giorgio. You may be right. Let's find a table where we can study it further."

They ordered coffee for which Giorgio paid and chose a suitable table by one of the windows, looking out over the boarding area, which all looked very peaceful in the early evening light, or at least until boarding time. They sat almost looking at each other over a square table with a big strategically placed vase right in the centre, filled with some sort of giant flowers. It was just in the right position. Giorgio chose the right table. It will stop him looking directly in to Francesca's face. Before he could say we should have something savoury with our coffee, Francesca moved the vase to one side, sat up straight, taking a deep breath, looked directly in to his eyes.

"Giorgio, now I can see you clearly. We should try to get to know each other. I'm very interested in your line of business." "You're right Francesca. I look forward to sharing new technological information with you. I believe it's something we may have in common. Excuse my sarcasm. You know we cannot talk about anything else but the weather." "Why do you say that Giorgio? We are only business acquaintances having coffee."

"Don't play me, Francesca. Let me get right to it; I believe you know my position? As I know yours, well certainly on the surface. You also know something is going on. What exactly? I'm not sure. I do know as you do that documents have been taken from the Athens office of social learning. Now, I don't see any point in me not talking openly and direct about what I know.

Stuff the protocol. We need to be upfront. This idle chit chat is ok, but it's getting us nowhere. Francesca, you need to take control of this growing situation from the so-called friendly group surrounding you by throwing a line at them." Giogio hesitated looking at Francesca for a reaction. She sat motionless holding his gaze. Giorgio went for broke. "Make it clear you will not be pushed around. You're aware of the situation, and you don't like it, just say it at the earliest opportunity."

He stopped. He could see she was deliberating on what he had said, not sure how she will take it, probably with a verbal reaction or physical. Francesca was still looking at him but still nothing. He decided that was enough. They needed to talk on a softer subject, if she stayed. "Francesca, I would be interested to hear more of your visit to Athens. A bit feeble I thought but it's the only place we both know."

Now, the strategic flowers had been moved Giorgio couldn't help but looked directly at Francesca, who was a very pretty, quietly attractive, dark-haired Italian, in her early thirties, slim, 5ft 4ish, spoke pretty good English, and with a good sense of humour. Probably a minor point, but Giorgio hadn't mentioned he was going to Cannes and the ship that must have been on their file, but not that he had moved on from that side of life.

They both sat looking at each other waiting for their coffee. Giorgio thought Francesca's probably wondering what he's thinking as he is looking at her facial expressions and in to her eyes. She's giving nothing away, that's experience, but then some women know how to keep a secret, until you get close.

Giorgio looked toward the boarding area. It was still quiet. Turning back, he saw Emilio admiring the view of the sharp business-suited Francesca from his vantage point at the far end of the bar, where he sat drinking coffee. Their order arrived, two large black coffees with complimentary wrapped biscuits on a small plate, no savoury sandwich. Francesca unwrapped one of the special assortment of biscuits, broke it in half eating one half. Giorgio continued looking at Francesc. She was still there.

"Giorgio, you should try the biscuit. They're very good, although I think you would have preferred something savoury. Never mind, the delegates' dinner will have something you like. Tell me, Giorgio. Do you know Athens very well? Have you walked through the centre?" "Not that often. When I do, it's mostly business, cafes, restaurants and the occasional club. I enjoy walking to most of these venues but not on this visit."

"As you only arrived on Monday, Giorgio, your time has been limited to meetings with other procedural duties, I know that now, whereas I have been here for eight days. It will save you checking. I have also followed a similar route—meetings, etc., I did have the odd half of a day free."

Giorgio listened to Francesca's in-depth visits around the city, places they had both been. They talked of its business, its social life, the acropolis tourism, how good the shops were, not for Giorgio though as he had very little interest in shops or shopping, unless it involved lunch or dinner with someone special. Francesca took control of the conversation with renewed enthusiasm, how she and her secretary toured round buying things. Giorgio recognised the shoe part as one pair were red. She lost him at the rest. He was sure he uttered agreement at the appropriate time on some items.

Francesca pointed out that they had to buy what sounded like bags and bags of whatever, as they were not available in Rome. Giorgio thought it appropriate for a light-hearted comment at this point, "You don't have to convince me. Francesca. You're free and single. Have fun. Two girls out and about shopping, I'm sure you found much to plan and discuss." Francesca replied with a slight smile and just a hint of a cheeky look. "We did, Giorgio. It's surprising how much information secretaries know. Isn't it Giorgio?" "Touché Francesca. I know where you're coming from." "Thank you, Giorgio. We seemed to have talked through the afternoon." Yes, Giorgio thought by who. Now, if the conversation had included some sort of technological system, which Francesca seemed to want to know earlier, that would have been interesting or even where her brother was. Nevertheless, he enjoyed their time.

Over two hours had slipped by, in that time, Giorgio noted Emilio had moved position twice, consuming several coffees, and the boarding area had become extremely busy, whereas the cafe was now practically empty. Francesca concluded the conversation and finished her coffee, looked at Giorgio for a moment and said, "I must go Giorgio." They both stood by the side of the table, parting with a handshake. Francesca gripping his hand just that little bit tighter, looked up at him with a very sharp-eyed look. "I have enjoyed our or my talking to you, paused briefly, and I have noted your comment, Giorgio." Letting go of his hand, "We shall see each other with our respective associates at the delegate's group dinner tonight so until then."

Giorgio stood watching as she slipped away and out of the cafe. Maybe, it was coincidence, their meeting at the harbour, both of them going to Rome. Giorgio would've liked to think so, but as often happens there's a motive. He thought. Is she working alone or for a third party? By the time you find out, something bad has happened further down the line, or even directly. Although Giorgio now had an insight in to Francesca's ways, he shall still have to be careful. She only has two full days. Adding that to the information he had learnt on the train, everyone seemed to be going their own way with their own agenda. The vast sums of money involved has created a power struggle that is splitting the group. It's not looking good. It's going to be a bad crossing. Giorgio tried to put it to one side for now but the idea of someone losing this power struggle was growing, worst of all is he knew everyone involved—who will win, who will fall. He left for the boarding area.

Chapter 7

The Crossing

Boarding as a foot passenger was all very straight forward. The luggage had already been taken aboard. Giorgio collected his cabin keys and headed off to the upper deck bar for coffee, making his way through a diligent crew and throng of passengers, all busy about their personal missions, against a red glowing evening sun, which pierced the angular styling of the ship with strange light orange shadows against its white painted superstructure, adding to the ambiance of machine noise, excited children and passenger chatter.

Entering the bar, you know exactly what part of the world you're in, as you step in to a stress-free atmosphere of tasteful Italian style decoration, square tables with chequered tops, seated mainly with similarly dressed grey-suited business types, some with their secretaries. Coffee and various flavoured multi-layered cakes was the main order, with no exception to Giorgio, making a good starter for the crossing. Staff were moving efficiently, back and forth with orders, making small talk. Giorgio chose a window seat with a good view overlooking the boarding area. Coffee arrived with his multi-layered chocolate cake. His instant thought: if this doesn't get to me, Francesca will, possibly not in a way I would want. He found his outer cabin with a sea view plain but comfortable. It's only fifteen hours. He unpacked the items needed for the crossing and decided to rest for half an hour by going over several reports. Lucia obtained for him, most pertaining to Antonio and Francesca with a note saying the main details he had requested would be waiting for him at Brindisi, finishing with, safe journey to you both, Giorgio, Lucia x. Good old Lucia. She wasn't old though, probably about Giorgio's age, but she acted and thought in a very mature way. It was her efficiency, and what a good cook! The slice of chocolate gateaux in the attaché case with the sandwiches were unbelievably delicious. Only one slice though.

55

Giorgio finished studying the report, writing in comments for Emilio to follow up; He'd noticed Emilio seemed to be playing an alternate role plan, reverting to his old self, a shadowy character as in the heavy days they enjoyed at sea. Giorgio recalled Angie's words, "You don't have to watch your back on this journey, just something else you don't have to think about, and it will give you the time you need to concentrate on the main issues."

Giorgio finalised his Middle East report complete with updates, which included details from Athens and information requests all completed, with his priority documents now locked in the attaché case, to be exchanged at Brindisi harbour with their internal courier service. Time for a refreshing shower and a change of clothes, something more appropriate for an evening meal with business associates.

The ferry was now clear of the dock. It felt good to be on board, and on his way back, he must be passing the harbour markers as a slight tremor came up through the ship, a familiar feeling he recalled, as her engines picked up power, heading out to the open sea.

It's odd he thought to be travelling by ship but not be involved in its operational duties, walking the decks as a passenger, with no control of its running. Then again, this is a commercial ship. Thank goodness. No more for him that environment. All he has to do here is arrive upright in Cannes, pass on what he knew, use up as much of the free time he had owing, which is considerable but so are the jobs, enjoy a good lunch with a few associates and start again after seventy-two hours or longer, if I can swing a small office task. It's time to relax and enjoy the evening, particularly as it's a warm pleasant evening. The beginning of spring should be ideal for deck strolling later. He looked out to admire the view as the harbour lights slowly diminished with the evening sun. Time for light refreshment from his tray of drinks before dinner and primarily meeting the unusually different Francesca, whom he suspects is his opposite number. She's following him for some important reason.

It's not for fun, and it won't end well. In fact, the whole scenario just doesn't make sense. He's ready for a good dinner and a positive night, but he can't stop thinking of all the new information. He keeps mulling over and over the reports in his mind, which have highlighted a few gaps in his thinking. He has a gut feeling that Emilio and he are being set up but he just can't put it together, and Francesca's tied in to this. Giorgio wonders if she fully understands. The more they talk the more he realises she is under some personal obligation or pressure or both from several so-called colleagues. He hope she thinks about his blunt words at the harbour cafe, or even acts on them. It would help or at least stir up a few emotions from others, maybe tonight will flush out more information. He thinks Emilio and he should talk before dinner, go over a few new ideas he has after reading the reports, a strategy of watching the associates and others, by keeping nearby, but not in an obvious way. Of course, it all depends on if any last-minute changes are made to the seating plan.

✳✳✳

The small dining area complete with its own bar was capable of seating one hundred and twenty people, and it had been fully reserved by the international financial group to provide for that amount, with ninety confirmed reservations, leaving room for additional guests on the night. Everything was catered for. Giorgio arrived to see Emilio with two secretaries and several others talking near the bar. The area was extremely busy with delegates milling around in groups, either waiting for friends or to be seated. Giorgio made his way over. "Giorgio, good evening," formally introducing himself to the secretaries and others, where they all stood discussing the last two meetings, land prices and oddly enough bonuses, which Giorgio noted from Emilio's hint of a smug expression they had topped theirs.

A waiter approached Emilio with good news. "We have your table ready, Emilio. We apologise for the delay. There have been slight changes to the seating plan." Only a slight change, the two secretaries were to the left of Emilio with Eva to Giorgio's right who he believed was already seated.

Giorgio was ready for something to eat; the bonus comments had added to his appetite. The waiter said "please follow me," and the waiter headed off. The four of them followed making their way round large pot palms and other big plants. The function organisers had gone through a lot of trouble by placing a mixture of large pot plants and low-level wicker screens to break the room up and provide atmosphere, as well as act as modesty panels, from indiscretions, no doubt.

Their reserved table was located at the far end where they sat with two finance groups in a semi-circle of tables, seated besides a mixture of ministerial, finance and private finance. They were seated opposite Francesca and Antonio, although two tables wide with a walkway in-between, probably just as well. Fortunately, the seating was right. Giorgio sat between Emilio and Eva, a little safer possibly. Eva, after a courtesy hello and a few minutes of small talk between the two of them, had gone round to talk with Antonio and Francesca, standing between the two of them.

It looked like a very frank and serious conversation. It stopped when Tullio appeared very unexpectedly with one of the finance ministers, both making their way to a table on the far side, where most of the private finance were seated. Eve and Antonio did not look pleased.

Emilio was discussing the last meeting agenda, in a light-hearted way, with the ministry secretary, who sat next to him and who appeared to be very attentive to his conversation. Emilio occasionally turned to ask Giorgio various pointers about the Cannes office's forthcoming itinerary of social meetings. Giorgio was glad that they discussed a few ideas of strategy before going into dinner.

Opposite the questioning conversation with Francesca looked even more tense and enquiring, as she was listening to her brother and Eva, occasionally looking across at me for what looked like she needed answers to their questions, Francesca looked agitated just for an instant. "She stood up" said something to Eva and her brother, leaving them both looking at each other in what Giorgio thought to be extreme embarrassment.

Francesca looked extremely beautiful in her evening wear, with her hair up as she made her way round the tables in a smooth confident way, hiding the irritation she must have felt. Giorgio could almost feel the energy from her as she passed behind him stopping by his side. He stood up next to her moving the chair; Francesca thanked him as she sat down. She turned to him. "Giorgio, please excuse me. I will be sitting here for this evening, not Eva. I hope you don't mind." She said with a hint of irritation in her voice.

Giorgio looked directly into Francesca's eyes for 3 or 4 seconds, replying, "It's always a pleasure to sit next to a beautiful woman." She stared into Giorgio's eyes replying, "Giorgio, I am not that nice," and I have several questions for you to which I apologise in advance as it is for my brother Antonio. "Then, please let me apologise in advance for I too would like answers to several questions. Are we in agreement?" "Yes." Francesca sat silently for a moment, turned to Giorgio with a frowned look saying, "Giorgio, we should talk now as the words of Eva and my brother are dancing in my head. You understand, I hope."

She wanted information that was not on this gathering's or Giorgio's agenda. Based on this, was only a social gathering not a fact-finding mission, and in particular not to outsiders who happen to arrive out of nowhere and ingratiate themselves to members of staff via a family member. Giorgio answered several questions with questions, starting with, what if, followed by, why.

The conversation became a frustrating farce. "Francesca, this is quite ridiculous. I have an altogether different proposal that might be good for both us and our departments." They agreed they did not trust each other, but something must be done. Fortunately, for both of them, they compromised as the starter for dinner arrived. They sat quietly occasionally looking at each other, enjoying the very sumptuous meal and very expensive wine. "Now, you can enjoy the savoury food you missed," she said smiling.

As the night progressed with good food, wine and brandy, Giorgio noticed the stiff-necked barriers starting to slip, with random risqué humour and raucous laughter from ministerial and private sector.

Even the not-so-nice Francesca had slipped a little, with her hair now slightly out of place. She boldly told Giorgio a risqué joke, which he secretly hoped he would remember.

"Francesca," Giorgio replied, "You do surprise me. Of course, I only know tame humour. You'll have to come closer. I shall whisper a couple of short verses to you." "Giorgio," she said laughing, "I thought mine were beyond risqué; you're very naughty." But she still giggled and laughed each time. Looking over the tables Giorgio noticed a few stiff glances to Francesca from Antonio and Eva. Halfway through the evening an uninvited Ponti joined them for a few minutes, all very curious and slightly disturbing. Giorgio glanced at Emilio, noting the familiar look that Emilio had the same thought.

Giorgio didn't think Francesca noticed. If she did, it was like putting two fingers up to them all for treating her with casual contempt. Nothing was going to stop her enjoying herself as Giorgio and Francesca talked almost non-stop for an hour, interspersed by Giorgio glancing at the odd goings-on here and there, brought on, no doubt, by the wine and brandy being so abundantly enjoyed by all. Francesca looked positively radiant; her long hair had slipped even more out of place laughing at, yet another of Giorgio's risqué jokes. She looked at Giorgio with her head slightly down, her eyes looking up into his, moving her head slowly side to side, saying, "It is not going to happen Giorgio." Giorgio took Francesca's hand saying, "Francesca, how could you think such a thing?" She just tilted her head giving Giorgio a hint of a smile with a very knowing look. Well, what could Giorgio say? He didn't even realise.

The whole party was in full swing. Everyone having a good time, making the most of this one-off get together, even those opposite to Giorgio and Francesca smiled between frowns at Francesca.

The gathering was purely for social reasons and goodbyes, as they would all be leaving for their hometown in one country or another. The night although still boisterously bright would be winding down in another hour. Emilio and the secretary he had conversed with for most of the evening made their goodbyes. Francesca, surprisingly, knew the girl as she stood up to say goodbye to her, a little disconcerting for Giorgio. Giorgio hoped Emilio noted the connection.

Giorgio watched as they left to see if anyone was interested in their departure before turning to Francesca, "Shall we go for coffee on the upper deck bar?" "What a good idea Giorgio!"

They said their goodbyes to all that counted. Giorgio noted the look on several faces as they left the table. Francesca took his arm as they navigated around the tables of high-spirited people enjoying the night, making their way toward the deck exit. Francesca turned to Giorgio. "It has been a beautiful evening Giorgio." The doors were opened for them. They went through out from the heady euphoric atmosphere of music and laughter on to the quiet deck on a warm clear night.

As the doors slowly closed behind them, the silence engulfed them both. Francesca leaned her head against Giorgio's shoulder saying, "I don't think this is what I expected, Giorgio. I'm not sure whether I should believe your plan, but if you're right?"

"Well, I think walking out before the end of the night may have had the desired effect we wanted for Eva and your brother, possibly others. I don't think it went down well that we left together, and that was a good move linking arms, Francesca. I would love to have turned to see their faces." "I did it because I wanted to hold your arm, Giorgio." They walked along the deck in silence; there was a warm breeze from the ship's forward momentum.

It was a clear starry night. Giorgio turned and held Francesca firmly with both hands, gripping her slim waist, kissing her on the cheek. Looking into Francesca's eyes, he could see a dreamy look of just one too many. "It might be best to leave coffee. We should both turn in, and take advantage of the few hours we have to sleep before the dawn overtakes us. It will help us keep a clear head. I shall see you back to your cabin." "Thank you, Giorgio, and stop using the phrases I do not know. Tell me what is turning in? Not tonight. I shall tell you when we have our next coffee or brandy."

"I might. I might not let you have coffee or brandy with me." Giorgio turned to reply, just catching a glimpse of Emilio ahead of them slightly in the shadows alone. Giorgio stood in front of Francesca looking at her face taking in all of her beautiful features. Francesca broke in to his thoughts. "Yes, Giorgio? You look as if you need an answer." Giorgio kissed Francesca on the cheek again and returned to her side, looking ahead. There was no sign of Emilio. He had evaporated in to the shadows again. "You wanted to say something. Didn't you Giorgio?" "Yes. I did but it can wait."

They continued walking along the deck, occasionally looking at each other. Francesca held Giorgio's arm, making the odd comment about other couples walking, how peacefully quiet it was, and how romantic the moon's reflection was on the beautiful calm sea. Giorgio agreed but couldn't help making the comment: its calm beauty can mesmerise you, but it could be a cruel unforgiving place to a ship. Many things have happened on the dark seas, and the deep oceans keep many secrets. They stopped walking.

Francesca turned and stood in front of Giorgio this time. "Giorgio, is it really so bad? Will you go back to your ship?" "No Francesca. Those days have gone. It was a short period in time but very intense. Your file is now updated."

"Giorgio, I didn't want to know for that reason, I'm interested in your, well I was just being personal. Tell me something of your ship, Giorgio, and the places you travelled to. Did you ever see action?" "Francesca, ships are personal, and no, we never saw any major action, although we did become involved in an incident." Francesca squeezed Giorgio's hand. "Ooo," she said, "tell me." "I can't tell you for official reasons, but I can quote a poem that is close to the way it was. Would you like to hear about a shadowy ship hunting a seized missile ship?" "Yes. Tell me, Giorgio," she said, gripping Giorgio's hand tighter. "On reflection, it might not sound so good." "Tell me, Giorgio. Tell me, please." "Mm well... Ok, I think this is from the middle. No, I remember the beginning. It's titled, The Commander. "That's it. No more tales of the sea tonight, but it's a reminder for me that it sometimes helps me to keep a clear head and focus, which is very difficult each time I look at you Francesca."

"You do not mean that, Giorgio, and I would like to hear more of your thoughts of that time. Can you write that verse down for me? Emilio said you have a verse written by you or your then fiancé, I cannot remember now, and is the ship really like your wife at sea or is it the ship protects you and keeps you safe at sea, and your wife keeps you safe and looks after you on land." "It's not real, Francesca, just a tall tale of the sea." "Giorgio, I don't believe you. I am not listening to you, and I will ask will you. Oh, I can't think. Would you, Oh Giorgio, when we are in the bright sunlight with a table between us, I will ask you then." "Why and what Francesca?" "You are being provocative Giorgio; you know why and what, and I won't look at you anymore."

They arrived at Francesca's door, where they both stood looking at each other. Francesca kissed the back of Giorgio's hand and held it on her cheek for a moment, with a searching look into his eyes, before saying in her soft broken English Italian way. "Goodnight Giorgio. It has been a beautiful evening" Her head tilted to one side and her hair now everywhere on to her shoulders and covering the side of her face. She looked so special. Giorgio wanted to pick her up in his arms and run away with her beyond the reach of either side. Such wishful thinking. Instead, all he could say was, "Good night, Francesca. Sweet dreams."

Giorgio left for his room. Stopping a short way down the corridor, he turned to Francesca and walked back. Francesca slightly the worse for wear was now leaning against her door looking at and thinking of Giorgio. His black hair, his chiselled features, and his brooding dark eyes that had a hard brightness about them. She slowly realised she was looking directly into Giorgio's eyes, who was stood in front of her. She quickly said, "yes," instantly realising she didn't mean to say that, and stood quietly looking into Giorgio's eyes.

Giorgio moved closer to Francesca, and keeping eye contact, he took her hand gently pulling her towards him. Francesca let herself be pulled into Giorgio's chest as his other arm held her round the waist. She was glad as she felt a little unsteady. Giorgio leaned forward inserted her key and unlocked the cabin door. Still looking at each other, Giorgio kissed Francesca lightly on the lips and moved back. Still holding her hand, he raised it and kissed her palm. They stood looking at each other, which seemed to last but it was only seconds. Giorgio placed the key into her palm, closing her fingers over it. He looked again into her eyes momentarily, saying, "You gave me your key to look after for you at dinner. I remembered halfway down the corridor." Francesca felt slightly flushed. Before she could put her thoughts straight to say anything, Giorgio thanked her for a wonderful evening. He leaned forward again kissing her on the cheek, and left.

Francesca continued standing by her now-open door, clutching her key, watching Giorgio make his way down the corridor and out of site. She sighed, went in, and closed and locked the door. She headed straight for the bed, climbed on to it, flicked off her shoes, pulled the bed cover over her and lay there fully clothed very tired and slightly drunk, feeling the ships movements and sounds. She thought of Giorgio, momentarily, possibly longer, as he moved dangerously in and around her mind slipping in to her thoughts as if she could feel him holding her firmly again as he had earlier. I mustn't think these thoughts she kept telling herself, as she drifted off to sleep.

Giorgio made his way back to the main deck where Emilio had signalled to meet and where he had conveniently disappeared for Francesca's sake. "Giorgio" he called from a deck storage door.

"What is it, Emilio?" "I have seen Ponte on the boat deck. Something is not right. Tullio was on the deck below talking with two or three associates. This area will become very busy soon, Giorgio. You and I need to find a spot and observe." "Which deck do you want, Emilio?" "I shall stay here. This is where Ponte was last time I saw him." "Ok. I'll go aft, give it thirty minutes and meet up by the main deck bar." "That's good, Giorgio."

As Giorgio headed for the aft deck, he passed several groups of passengers and a small group of delegates still in good high spirits spilling out from the dining room. The party was coming to a gradual end. Glancing in, he noticed it was still very busy with at least half the total of delegates still going strong or unable to stand. It all looked good. Continuing aft, it had become very quiet. Giorgio heard a couple of voices coming from the restricted crew only area of the aft deck, probably members of the crew. He moved closer. It wasn't the crew. He climbed over the perimeter rails. It was Eva and Tullio arguing. Eva was gesturing, shouting, and hitting out at Tullio, who punched Eva. Grabbing her bag as she fell backwards hitting the deck hard, to Giorgio's amazement and Tullio's, she swung a metal bar at his leg. He jumped back pulling a knife. Eva moved back. Giorgio ran forward as Tullio stabbed at Eva. Giorgio grabbed at Eva with one hand, and still moving forward, hit Tullio hard and square with the other, a fist to the neck. Giorgio heard something. He went down. Still holding the knife, Eva cried out as the knife pulled out of her shoulder. Looking at Giorgio all she said was, "Giorgio." Giorgio just managed to get an ungainly grip of her, lowering her on to the deck. Eva sat dazed on the deck, as he supported her looking at her face and into her eyes to see if she was going to stay with him and not pass out. "Eva try and relax while I check the wound." He pulled Eva's top off the area. There was enough light from the overhead winch lights to see that it was ok with very little blood. "Eva you'll be fine but I need to get you to the upper deck. A medic who's patched up more wounds than you've had whatever. Have you got a hanky or anything clean to hold over it?" "In my bag. Oh, it is over there by that rope on a bin," she said shakily. "Where do you mean?

Oh, the winch by Tullio. What have you got in this Eva? An armoury? I can feel a barrel." He said as Giorgio handed it to Eva. "It's just a little protection, Giorgio. Here, is this all right?" "Silk, have you got any clean tissues?" "Yes, here you are." "That's better. It's just to keep it clean and stop the small amount of blood getting everywhere, and the night insects getting in." "Giorgio, I can walk all right if you can support me." "Hold on to the rail. I want to check Tullio" Giorgio stood and checked him over. had one on his neck while trying to pull himself up to a sitting position. Giorgio sat him up against the winch, had a few words and went back to Eva saying, "He's going to walk out of here shortly. What do you want to do? Call someone or leave him? We're on a ferry, Giorgio. Where can he go?"

"That's not a good answer but I'm going to let him know." Giorgio knelt by Tullio letting him know Eva's answer. "Tullio, I'd make tracks if I were you. You've got a fifty, fifty chance more than you gave others." Giorgio made him stand up, and he grabbed his jacket sleeve. Giorgio crouched down again without a word. He delved in to a deep inner pocket. Pulling out a rolled pouch, he thrust it in to Giorgio's hand and pushed him away. Giorgio stood up putting it in to his jacket without looking back. He checked on Eva, put his arm round her waist for support and they made their way to the bar where Emilio would be.

He left Eva to sit at one of the bar tables holding the tissue, and he walked over to Emilio. "You ok, Giorgio." "I'm fine." "Who was it?" "Tullio, I left him on the aft deck with a stiff neck but he's ok. I imagine he's made himself scarce after I told him what Eva said that he had nowhere to go. Can you sort out a shallow knife wound to Eva's shoulder? She's holding a tissue on it for now." "Giorgio, before I go over to Eva, we should talk before we disembark." "Ok, make it here." "I wouldn't stay with her too long. Antonio or Ponte will be looking for her." "Emilio, before I go. Tullio gave me a rolled pouch I put it straight in my pocket. I didn't want Eva to see; we need to check it now." "Ok, let's have a look." "There's another flat pouch. Look at this, Emilio. It's unbelievable—a jewelled necklace, a real classic." Giorgio passed it to Emilio. "Giorgio, this is a one-off; it must be priceless." "There are several keys in this small pouch, Emilio. You hang on to the necklace. I'm going down to check Tullio's cabin." They put the pouches away and both walked back to Eva. Emilio removed the tissues. "It could do with clipping. Eva, is it ok for me to clean the wound and put a dressing on?" "Of course, Emilio. I thought it would be you. I will have it re-dressed at Brindisi when we arrive."

"Giorgio, I'm going for the keys to the first-aid room." Giorgio sat next to Eva. Want to tell me what it was about Eva?" "It was an internal matter, Giorgio. It will be seen to. It had to be you that stopped Tullio. Why did you, Giorgio."

"Maybe, it's because you have a new life ahead or I didn't like Tullio, pick one of those." "Giorgio, I have the keys." "I shall leave you in Emilio's good hands. See you later, Emilio." Giorgio headed off to his cabin.

"Giorgio," Eva called out.

Giorgio turned to her. She looked at him with those big eyes. Well, they weren't that bad. He replied, "Eva."

"Thank you, Giorgio. Ponti and I owe you."

Giorgio noted she tried to smile as he did. He nodded and left.

✳✳✳

The night was soon gone. Waking to the sound of a ship's horn, Giorgio sat up looking out at the shoreline and watched a large freighter low in the water heading out to sea. It gave another short blast of its horn. Time to get ready Giorgio thought. The ferry port wasn't too far off, maybe forty-five minutes. He showered and prepared everything for the day ahead, with bags packed ready for collection. It left plenty of time for coffee before coming along side. It would also be a good opportunity to see who was up and about. He made his way top side by way of the grand style internal stair case. It came out on to the sun deck. The cafe looked quiet as he walked over to the ship's rail, enjoying the overall view as we followed the Italian coastline heading towards the port of Brindisi, with the usual accompaniment of seabirds who were also enjoying the clear blue sky and early morning sun by ducking and diving around the ship, a good warm start to the day and spring, a real feel good factor.

Giorgio noted a few people exercising on the aft deck. No one he recognised from last night's bash. They were probably still under the bedcovers. Emilio was heading to the café. Giorgio called out and walked over, top of the morning. "Emilio, so how did it go last night."

"I patched her up ok and sent her off to her cabin where she probably met up with Antonio. She was not too happy with you, Giorgio, for swinging Francesca over to us. I can't think why, still it's only a minor problem to everything else that's happened, but you will like this Giorgio, she was very grateful that it was you who saved her; I think you may have made a friend of your enemy." "Thanks Emilio. I bet you egged her on as well." "Well, Giorgio, anything for a friend, and Giorgio, I studied the necklace. I am convinced it belongs to Francesca's family, stolen by Antonio. I have looked at the hallmarks, and I am sure it was made in London in the 1920s. I will check when I go ashore." "Well done, Emilio. It's all beginning to make sense. I paid a visit to Tullio at his cabin. He was out for whatever reason, which is not good. I took the opportunity to go through everything before anyone else did. I found several old newspaper cuttings—one was of Antonio and Francesca offering a reward for missing jewellery.

Tullio knew Antonio had the necklace and stole it from him. I also have papers regarding artwork sales and auctions, which may be of interest for you and central, but the keys, I think, they belong to a deposit box. There was nothing in the cabin like that and certainly not now." "Why do say that, Giorgio?" "I walked past his cabin earlier. It has been totally ransacked, and I think we know who and why." "Giorgio, it puts you and me, possibly Eva, in a bad situation." "Emilio, as you're going ashore first, you better take all of Tullio's bits and pieces, which is in a grey holdall hanging on the back of my cabin door. It also includes fourteen thousand US dollars in small bills. One of your contacts will come up with something, and you can pay with Tullio's money. Francesca and I will watch from up here. I'm interested to see who disembarks." "Ok Giorgio. I will see you at the station. Be vigilant. They may go for Francesca." Giorgio went in to the café, ordered coffee and sat on the seaward side, listening to the light music and looking out at distant ships, mostly coastal freighters, two big container ships heading through the Mediterranean too far off ports, and one grey ship bristling with aerials and other interesting bits and pieces; she looked very capable of looking after herself going in a hurry to who knows where. All very interesting, Giorgio thought, but time wasting, and left to organise collection of their bags.

Returning to his cabin Giorgio met Francesca in the main corridor. "Good morning Francesca." She stopped in front of him, looking just a little tired, and gave him a smile. "Giorgio. Last night, I have several questions, we must talk." "When we dock, if that's ok, Francesca? I've organised a porter to take our bags ashore. I thought it would be safer if we kept everything together easier for both of us to keep an eye on each other's bags." "All right, Giorgio. All my things are ready. I shall wait on the deck for you. Now, I will go for coffee on the upper deck." "Ok Francesca. I need to collect my attaché case. I'll see you top side in five minutes." "I know that saying Giorgio. I heard one of the crew say the same so I asked him; I thought you might say it," she said smiling. She gave a little wave still smiling as she left. Giorgio arrived at the upper deck lounge as Francesca came out and called to him. "Hello Giorgio" and waved. She walked over, took Giorgio's hand and kissed him on the cheek. "I've finished my coffee. Let's look over the town." They both stood leaning on the heavy wooden topped railing. "Two things Francesca, I like your wave and smile." "I know it's a little silly, it's just that I like to when we meet or part. You don't mind. Do you Giorgio?" I hope you never stop Francesca, and I like it when we say hello with a kiss. "Oh, Giorgio. It's just a social greeting. Nothing personal. I don't even know you. Well not. Oh, let's change the subject. It's a beautiful day, Giorgio. The dock looks so busy. You would be used to seeing it like this. Is it just another dock to you, Giorgio, all these people bustling about?" "No Francesca. Some are more important than others. Is this one, Giorgio?"

"This one is of special importance, Francesca." Giorgio said looking out over the docking area. He spotted Emilio in the crowd, talking with several delegates from last night. Everything up to now was under control. For how long he thought, he hadn't seen Antonio or Ponti leave the ferry by foot or Tullio and Eva. It's a bit worrying, all four dropping out of sight, maybe something's happened. "Giorgio, what are you thinking. You're so quiet." "Oh, I'm sorry, Francesca. I was deep in thought with what is happening about us, the nature of our business. I'm trying to keep myself in focus, trying to second guess where everyone is. I know it's early and to the point but we need to keep right on the ball. Something serious is going down, involving all three of us. You need answers to some very serious questions, that involve Emilio and me, and you're in the middle, which is very worrying and frustrating. There's a lot at stake. Your brother and others have a lot to lose. All of us have a lot to lose, and someone is going to pay one way or another."

"All right, Giorgio. I understand it all too well and its madness. Why are you here? Why do you have to be involved? I'm sorry but I am sick of it all, and don't say anything, Giorgio. I'm going in the cafe for another coffee." "Wait Francesca," Giorgio took her hand. "It will be ok." Francesca came forward and put her arms round Giorgio's waist, "I know it will, Giorgio. I just wanted you to tell me." Giorgio kissed her on the cheek, another twenty-four hours to Rome. Francesca kissed him on the cheek, then turned and headed to the cafe. She stopped by the door, "Giorgio, will you have a cappuccino?" "Yes, I'll have a pastry as well since you're paying."

They remained on board, waiting for the crowds to thin out before they disembarked, collecting their luggage dockside. "Francesca, I think, we should eat here at the port unless you know of somewhere else as this is your turf." "Oh, Giorgio. What do you mean turf?" Giorgio explained and also the meaning of turning in, adding, "If we trusted each other a little more, we could spend our time talking about each other and all these quaint and quirky little sayings. Sadly, a lot of our time is spent on our own protection, covering ourselves as we go forward, but you can tell me what your travel plans are or whatever your able to. We need to figure out what their next move is and hopefully be one step ahead."

⋙⟨⟩⋘

Chapter 8

Brindisi

Francesca chose the cafe where they sat quietly enjoying their continental breakfast in a pleasant atmosphere of light early morning music, surrounded by several of the revellers of last night, all looking very under the weather, even Francesca still looked a little tired. "Giorgio, I will go for the car now. I will not be long. The car is only a few minutes away, maybe we can talk more when we are at the station. We need to talk." Giorgio ordered another coffee. His courier would be in as soon as Francesca left. "Giorgio, look after my attaché case; I have locked it." Francesca smiled and gave her little wave.

Giorgio watched her smooth way of walking in her now-favourite red shoes, which as she told him in Patras, she had bought in Athens after their first meeting. She left the cafe to collect her car from maybe the port car park or from someone. Giorgio wondered at her last words, "We need to talk." It could be business, but he had heard those words before. The company courier came in, carrying the discreetly logoed travel bag for him as he sat pondering the day ahead while waiting for Francesca's return, which could be ten minutes or more. The courier left after their quick change over, giving him time for a look in the travel bag and to finish his coffee, just in time to see Francesca getting out of a red saloon car in front of the café.

She came in smiling. "Giorgio, you are ready to go? Pointing to her watch, she said, "I was only ten minutes. I bet you thought I would be longer." They arrived at the station. Francesca pulled in to the short-stay car park, where a porter collected their bags, following them in to the station concourse. Francesca already had her ticket booked from Athens—a 1st class sleeper; they headed for the ticket office. Francesca confirmed her booking and location of the compartment, which was near the front end of the train. Giorgio tried for a last-minute couchette without success. Only shared compartments were available, Emilio, his shadow as Giorgio came to call him, who was always strategically around, walked in to the ticket office. "Any luck Giorgio? "Nothing." "Let me talk to them." "Ok Emilio. We shall be in the cafe across the way. Emilio, before you go, did you see Tullio before or after we disembarked?" "No, the last time was at the dinner. Of course, that was the last time I saw him as well."

"Well Giorgio," Francesca said standing in front of Giorgio, taking hold of his hand and still looking a little tired. "Thank you for coffee, Giorgio, again. I think that was in a dream of mine that maybe we should have coffee together but no brandy. Is that right?" She said looking at Giorgio, and smiled. She continued, "I'm glad we talked. Thank you for listening. I have to park the car and visit relatives. I will see you here 1 hour before departure." She kissed Giorgio on the cheek, keeping eye contact that lingered for a moment, and she then left, disappearing for half a day. Under normal circumstances ok, not here though, Giorgio felt a slight apprehension again, but he had to go along with it, what else could he do. Emilio came in waving goodbye to Francesca, "Well Giorgio. I have a 4-berth compartment for two, a little persuasive influence." "Well done, Emilio. Let's have an early lunch. We can go through the courier papers, and take a look round the town later." After visiting several shops for electrical components, as well as one café and two restaurants collating and pooling their various bits of information, they headed back to the station. It all turned out well with Francesca off, visiting her relatives or wherever. Emilio came up with an idea worth trying.

The train was in, and the platform gates were open. Passengers were commencing to board. Emilio headed off to find the compartment and organise their luggage and the electrical items purchased on their afternoon in town.

Giorgio met up with Francesca at the station café, after she had apparently parked the car and visited relatives, maybe it was true. They kissed each other on the cheek, such a good custom he always thought, albeit maybe a little false on this occasion, or was it? They made their way to the platform stopping briefly to buy chocolates and a paper before heading off to the first-class carriages. The station and gate area leading on to the platform was surprisingly quiet; They passed through and walked in silence up the platform. Several thoughts passed through Giorgio's mind, one, whether to ask about her brother, and would he be joining her, also what the outcome had been regarding Eva and Tullio; he thought better of it for now, anyway.

"You're very quiet again, Giorgio. Is it business? "Yes, it is but the answers I need you will not be able to give, or you just won't know the answer. This is your carriage." Francesca turned to Giorgio with a worried frustrated look. "Giorgio, I want to help but I have no answers. I don't know where anyone is. They have not been in touch; maybe, they are avoiding me after my words with them at the delegates dinner. It's very disturbing and upsetting." They stepped up into the carriage. Giorgio's compartment was in the middle, between the wheels. They arrived at the door as the porter was leaving after putting all of their bags in the compartment. Francesca thanked him and went in. Putting her bag on the table, she turned and looked at Giorgio. He avoided Francesca's look. "It's more spacious than I expected."

"Yes Giorgio. It's all right. I am not going to ask you anything; I look into your eyes to assure myself." Francesca busied herself moving the bags to the sides and into a cupboard, eventually satisfied with the outcome, they sat at the table in comparatively comfortable surroundings with all the amenities of first class. Francesca stood up now, "I know where everything is. I shall make us a drink." They sat having their coffee. "One slight problem, Francesca, entry between 1st and 2nd class is usually locked. I shall look at it from the other side later." "Yes, I understand Giorgio. It is a little awkward." As I am booked as a single, Francesca told me, and you're booked in to the four-berth compartment, you would need to be in your compartment for the attendant to take and confirm the head count to confirm all ticket holders were accounted for. "It's not a problem, Francesca. Just keep your door locked. Emilio and I have things to do."

"All will be well, Giorgio. I have plenty to do as well." For some reason, Francesca had been a good ambassador with everything up to now. Giogio hoped it continued, as he was leaving his bags here both unlocked for an important reason. They contained files to help Francesca understand those close to her, both cases had a few personal items of his which might be of interest, and he was sure she wouldn't be able to resist looking through everything. His other bag and attaché case would have been stowed away by Emilio in their compartment. "Francesca, it's time for me to get back. I need to see who's around and make things happen."

She took Giorgio by the hand saying, "I shall hope to hear from you later, Giorgio." She stopped. "Francesca, all will be well." "Thank you, Giorgio, but I need to say, please be careful." She kissed him on the cheek again, saying, "it's just protocol, Giorgio." Did she mean it? Was it protocol? Men are often kept guessing. It's best to take no notice as this journey wasn't over yet by a long way. Giorgio left the carriage, making his way down the platform, wondering what the next move would be. With no sign of their key players and time slipping away, would they make an attempt to get at Francesca, probably unlikely, unless Eva still felt bitter, although with her injury, maybe not, the likely targets would be Emilio or myself, Ponti and Antonio would know of my talk with Tullio, Eva would have told the whole story she may have seen me slipping something in to my jacket? With Tullio mysteriously missing who has the stolen documents? Giorgio stood at the compartment door still mulling over all the available information, wondering what would come of this journey.

He knocked on the side window calling out to Emilio and opened the door. Emilio was busy with the intruder transmitter, "How's it going?" "It's all working ok. I have just finished covering everything. The train attendants will be calling in soon, checking reservations. We don't want them to see our modifications to the compartment." Giorgio opened and closed the door to check activation on the receivers. "Just testing, they're both working ok. Good timing. Well done, Emilio." "Giorgio, this is your earpiece and receiver. When the door opens, it will beep three times, and you will hear whatever is happening in the compartment. The volume control is on the side of the receiver." "Ok what else is there Emilio? You're looking too pleased with yourself." "While you were with Francesca, I spoke with the train superintendent about currency and passengers. I have the compartment number of Antonio.

He used his real name luckily for us; maybe, we should pay a visit, social, of course." "Let's be a little subtle Emilio. We should at least wait until the train is clear of the station. We don't want him to jump off before we have the papers, if he has the papers." Emilio did like to go directly to the source, but then sometimes, throwing caution to the wind does pay off, and for some reason or another, Emilio is returning to Rome, it must be some official reason, not sure what yet? Although, Giorgio was glad. He thought it's good to have a heavy weight backing you up, as an ex-boxer and rugby player, he's just the person you need. Thinking back, Emilio was always a very handy heavyweight to have around. Their early days often seemed more chaotic, more urgent, always things to be dealt with, travelling here and there, getting the job done one way or another, meeting up at some official gathering, talking of the latest exploit and enjoying the odd bottle of whatever was on offer or available. It was never boring and nothing seems to have changed much, even with Emilio's now new official position. Mind you if they wanted a coffee here and now, to reach the buffet you would have to battle your way through 4 coaches of passengers, families, friends, all spilling into the corridors, although many of the people on the train were not passengers, just friends and family saying their goodbyes. Most will be gone when the train leaves. Francesca, on the other hand, was alone, albeit in comparative comfort, hopefully safe and looking after or into Giorgio's luggage.

Someone knocked at the door. "It will be the attendant Giorgio," Emilio called out. The attendant replied with his name. Emilio let him in and shook his hand. They said a few words. The attendant left. "It's good to have someone on the inside, Giorgio. The attendant has knocked and checked Antonio's compartment. No one is there. I'm all finished here, Giorgio." "Good. I'm going to the station office to see the courier. For last-minute details, we only have fifteen minutes twenty tops." "Ok Giorgio. I will come down the platform in about 10 minutes. We can work our way up the train coach by coach together and see whose where. Giorgio made his way down the platform. Emilio checked his handy work on the compartment door and locked it. He turned and saw them on the far side of the platform, three of them. He watched; it was Antonio. He was gesticulating to one of the others, it looked like Ponte, and now both were waving their arms about. They were moving slowly across the platform away from the train.

Emilio made his way of the train and stood by the carriage door trying to keep them in sight. Giorgio wouldn't be back for another ten or fifteen minutes. He made the decision to follow them, making his way cautiously across the platform, recognising the third man now that he was closer. It was one of the private financial associates from Athens, but he couldn't remember his name, the other was Ponte all right, a heavy weight go between for the finance group, not a pleasant type, he was showing exactly that, it was all turning ugly, Emilio was close, it was night the station was lit but shadowy, with luggage box trucks parked here and there which Emilio made use of. Antonio was now shouting, accusing both of them at playing a double-dealing game, to acquire millions of dollars funding for gas oil and land deals using Francesca's security clearance. "It was you Ponte and Tullio trying to push me out by keeping all the documents to verify yourself, blaming me along with Giorgio for the loss of papers instead of just Giorgio, who was going to be the fall guy. We would both be eliminated. You shits would have got the credit and the money from selling the information to the highest bidder." "You're talking crap Antonio. It was you who started all this," Ponte shouted, "it was Tullio who forged the details for you and your so-called sister."

"Ponte, it is you who is talking crap," Antonio shouted back, "haven't you made enough money already without trying to squeeze me out?" Emilio moved forward toward Antonio, who pulled a gun. "Back off Emilio. Get back over the other side by the train. It would be a shame for you to spend your last breath on a platform." Emilio backed away slowly. "As for you Ponte, it's time you cooled down. We're all going to take a walk." The financier turned on both Antonio and Ponte, calling them low-level dirt, "Antonio, it was Ponte who tried to take over, threatening me for his own greed. It's total madness. There is plenty for all of us; you have both spoiled everything, when Eva finds out none of us will have anything." "Enough of your shit talk," Antonio shouted, "you're both getting on the train with me now."

Ponte and the financier turned. Antonio started to walk across the platform oblivious to Giorgio walking up the platform. As Giorgio got close, he called out to Antonio, who saw Giorgio's angry hardened face then saw the gun. He turned and headed off to the front of the train. Giorgio couldn't do anything about it. The other two were in the way, and a wasted shot here, would attract unwanted attention.

"Ok. You two stop where you are," Giorgio shouted. They stopped, both looking at the gun, they both spoke, "It was Antonio; we only financed it all. We are not involved in anything else." "Ponte, I almost believe you, except I know you're a backstabbing killer; your last victim Tullio was fished out of the water earlier. You killed Tullio," the financier shouted. "Don't put it on me. Check it out Giorgio. It was Antonio. Tullio tried to take over everything, after forging Francesca's security documents, giving him access to the security area at the offices of social learning, and then trying to involve Eva." "Ok Ponte. I can verify that it cross-references with what I already know, but you bastards involved me. I don't like that I don't like you. I will find Antonio and show him my displeasure for involving me in this scam, now lower the attaché case and step back. I will not ask twice, and you both have much to lose if you don't." Giorgio stepped back a reflex to Ponte's uneasy move. He stopped. The financier lowered the attaché case. They both stepped back. Giorgio had seen Emilio near the luggage trucks and called out. "Emilio, get the attaché case." The guards whistle blew and the train was about to go.

Giorgio waved them further back as Emilio lifted the attaché case, carefully noting to himself how heavy it was, not something to just tuck under your arm. He ran for the train. Giorgio was shouting at Ponte to take his financier and explain to his backers and Eva if he could, as he also ran to the train jumping on. Emilio was stood by the door. They both watched with amusement to see the financier gesticulating at Ponte, knowing the trouble they were both in. Emilio gave a loud "well-done" to Giorgio that was the best timing ever. Just happened to be in the right place at the right time, and we have the attaché case, and I can't wait to see what's inside." They headed for the compartment.

"Emilio, can you open the attaché case without damaging it? I have a feeling all the original documents are in it. I'm going to see if there's any way to get through to the first-class carriages. I'll be back in 5 to 10 minutes with coffee. Emilio, be careful as you probably heard me say on the platform Antonio killed Tullio."

Giorgio made his way slowly through the busy coach corridors thinking Antonio could hide anywhere any compartment, that's if he's on the train. He reached the end of the last second-class carriages. There was no chance of getting through. It was the guard's room and luggage compartment. He went in to check. The guard's door and the dividing carriage doors were locked. Giorgio made his way to the buffet car.

Emilio headed off to the back of the train, halfway down the corridor. Antonio came in at the end of the corridor, and Emilio ran head on to him using the attaché case against his chest as a ram. Antonio pulled a gun shouting "stop Emilio." Before he could do anything, Emilio shouted "bastard," crashing into him at the end of the corridor. Emilio tried to pin him to the wall; Antonio fought back like a mad man. Both struggled. Antonio trying to push Emilio to the open carriage door. The gun Antonio was holding slowly levelled at Emilio's body and fired. Emilio hit the wall. Giorgio came through from the other carriage at the exact moment dropped the coffee. They looked at each other, instantly Giorgio screamed out at Antonio, "You son of a bitch," as he lunged forward and grabbed at the gun smashing into Antonio. They fought. The gun fired again. Giorgio leaned back on the open door. Antonio looked for an instant at Giorgio holding his gun and fell backwards, holding his stomach, falling out on to the track in front of a southbound express.

Giorgio knelt to help Emilio who was now seated on the floor and looked up at Giorgio. "That bastard ruined a very expensive agency metal-lined attaché case, and it's given me a hell of a stomach-ache and back-ache." "You bastard, Emilio. He should have aimed at your thick skull. You frightened the hell out of me; you ought to buy me a drink. Come on you big jerk. Let's get you up and get you back to the compartment if you're up to it." "The compartment will be good, Giorgio." "We only just made it Emilio. It's a good job you didn't need carrying. I would have had to leave you there by the exit door. You might be reasonably fit but you're bloody heavy." "I was carrying the metal attaché case." "All right. Do you want to lay on the bunk or sit?" "Sit, Giorgio." "Just as well, I don't want you laying around feeling sorry for yourself, especially now with lots to do. I suppose you want a drink now." "Thanks Giorgio and a sandwich." "Don't push it."

"Pity about Antonio, definitely not a good time to get off. We could have all done with a few more answers. What do say, Emilio?" "Pour me another glass, Giorgio. I could do with another one as well and one of those sandwiches. I can't see any point in stopping the train either. I don't think first-aid will help. Christ, Giorgio, you're more hard-faced than I am, but you're right. Damn right, he didn't think twice about you.

Mind you, he did us all a favour by getting rid of Tullio. I'm glad they pulled Tullio out of the water. It could have put you off lobster in this area if they hadn't. Still a few agencies will be glad to see the back of him. Tetelestai as they used to say, Giorgio, paid in full." "Yes, he did. Didn't he? But I can't muster any sympathy for him, the grief he caused and for very little reason on some occasions. Apart from us getting the necklace and whatever else from the deposit box keys, tell you what Emilio that carriage door being open and Antonio being there, makes me feel he was waiting for one of us, we will never know for sure, but I think it was me when he found out that Tullio had given me the necklace somehow." "Well Giorgio. It was considerate of him to open the door." "Emilio, you're sounding better already but how are you feeling, as it's been an hour and cost me two bottles of their best wine." "Only half good, Giorgio. You drank one bottle." "Good,

I'm glad you're feeling 100 percent. You can get that attaché case open now any way you like, as it's damaged. Good job. It wasn't a booby trap case, and we still don't know for sure what's inside. If it is the missing files, we need a note of the top two essential individuals with any company names and contact numbers, and their account details passwords. We may need those as soon as we arrive in Rome, just in case we have an unwelcome committee at the station. If all's well, I shall get three full copies of everything for you and I and Francesca for future insurance. Emilio, if you follow my drift, and time is getting on when you've finished, we should clear our compartment, leave everything in the attendant's room, as you already know him, it ought to be safer there than locking it in here. We can pick it all up when we arrive."

"Giorgio, I will offer the attendant a little inducement as we don't want any unwanted attention like why he is storing passenger's bags. Mind you, Giorgio. They're going to be busy when we stop the train." "You're right, Emilio. I wonder what they will make of it. Anyway, I'm going to clear Antonio's compartment. See you back here with his gear; if there's a lot, it can go in with our bags."

"Is that it, Giorgio, one big case?" "No. There's an attaché case inside it. He was travelling light who knows why there was nothing else in the compartment, and considering what's in the case, I'm surprised he wasn't travelling first class. He should have asked you to book his compartment if there was no space left." "Maybe he didn't trust Francesca, Giorgio." They laughed. "It's a fair point, Emilio. We shall never know why. The attaché case has several files full of what looked like a mixture of business and personal information—three passports one automatic with several spare clips, plus a large amount of cash in both bags, US Dollars and mixed currencies. All the dollars were in money sacks of fifty thousand dollars, total six sacks over three hundred thousand. I don't know how much in mixed currencies, probably pay offs and expenses, same money sacks as in Tullio's on the Athens train. I saw Eva's name and Antonio's name on several documents, but if Francesca has read the documents in my luggage, she won't be that interested with anything of his. How you feeling now?" "Good. Thanks Giorgio. I found copies of the missing official documents, which were obviously being used to compromise you, Giorgio, and others to sell on to various international financial investors.

All this information was now worth a fortune, so much for the so-called good brother, not so good for Francesca on one side, but on the other, I think Francesca is in it up to her neck." "I have the same thoughts, Emilio." "We should be a little wary of Francesca. I take it she is not fully aware of her so-called brother's past yet, Giorgio." "She should know by now. It was all in my bags, which she has, and Emilio, I have a gut feeling she assisted in the entry of the social offices; she knows their protocol. She has the pass, and according to the secretary I met at the company party, she said her boyfriend who works as a security guard told her for money, etc. that Antonio accompanied her one time only. So, by showing Antonio around, he was able to write down the entry procedures and use Tullio to copy Francesca's security details pass and passwords and whatever else. There are copies of security passes in the attaché case.

This has been planned well in advance with all the names and contacts involved." "So, Giorgio, do you think it was a family dilemma with Francesca being sucked into this scam by the so-called dedicated half-brother to placate the family by bringing him back in to the inner circle or the more obvious solution she did it for money?" "It could be both, Emilio, but what she didn't know was that he had been bleeding the family or two members of the family for years, getting away hundreds of thousands in various currencies. It was all in the reports from central, which Francesca will have read by now as it was in my bags in her compartment, but with recent events and his ambitious plan of financial deception and probably many other things, they the family will be glad he has gone. When this becomes known, there will be questions regarding access to the Athen's offices, that's why Tullio was brought in to sort out the access documents and cards.

Did Eva have access, Emilio, and should we be interested as she's disappeared and Tullio has gone? I'm wondering Emilio if we should turn in all the documents to our people as most of the information was to be used against our section. The money or part of it can be used in conjunction with our completion arrangements." "Yes, I like that idea, Giorgio. Let's sort the paperwork into the correct attaché cases." "Which case has the mixed currencies in Emilio? We need to prepare that, and I want to put a note in with it. Emilio, if you're in agreement, it would be good for the family to put the necklace in with the currencies and my note, what do you think?" "I agree with you, Giorgio; it should be returned to the family. It will give them a chance to recover after all these years and start again." "Emilio, all the bags need to go with you. We can sort the big items now, and anything else on the second part of the journey to Cannes."

"Ok Giorgio. Everything is clear. You have the grey-marked attaché case with four sacks in; I have the black-ribbed attaché case with four sacks in. Both attaché cases to go in one bag with the remaining money for completion pay-outs and central." "Nice job, Emilio. Now, we can pass on the information to Francesca tonight in the grey attaché case with one sack, and I will take copies when we arrive and get them sent to central." "This is good for us, Giorgio, as we're all involved and she's their controller. We don't want repercussions from the other side, so the sooner Francesca passes on all this information the better."

Chapter 9

The Rome Express

"Ok. If you're ready Emilio, pull the emergency cord." Giorgio took the attaché case. The train came slowly to a halt. They both jumped to the ground. It was eerie running up the side of the train. Fortunately, it was a clear night, enough to keep their footing as they made their way towards the front, checking the 1ˢᵗ class carriage numbers. It was the second carriage from the front. Giorgio jumped up on to the steps, reached up and tried the door. It was unlocked, thank goodness.

They climbed up into the carriage and closed the door. "Before we go any further Emilio, let's have some sort of plan. I need to speak with Francesca, but I think it would be better if you go in first. All the information is in your attaché case. I have a feeling Francesca will be glad to talk, especially to you. I'll go to the restaurant and wait there for you; it will give me a chance to sort out our paperwork and reports." Emilio made his way along the corridor; it was the last cabin. He knocked, and the door opened. Francesca stared at Emilio. Her smile faltered to a worried look, "Is Giorgio with you? I am sorry, Emilio. Come in sit down." "Thank you, Francesca."

"Giorgio is fine. I'm very sorry Francesca. Things have been brought to a head. I know you were told, and you must have considered we, Giorgio, and I, were involved with the missing documents, and quite understandably that was their plan. Take my attaché case; it has all the documents taken from Antonio and his two associates, one you know, Ponte. The three of them were on the platform. The information it contains will explain almost everything—those involved and most importantly why."

"Where are they? Are they on the train Emilio? "No." "I'm glad Antonio is not here on the train." "Francesca, I will explain the details of tonight's events in more detail after you have seen the missing documents from the social learning offices and read the details on all the accompanying documents of finances, with names of those involved and other items in the case. It all lead to a platform confrontation, Tullio being shot on the ferry, your brother and I in a standoff and Giorgio saving my life." "Oh, Emilio, I have failed you and Giorgio." "Do not say that Francesca. It is not true. Just read the documents. We will talk afterwards. I can leave you for a time, and come back in thirty minutes or longer." "No. Stay Emilio, and I might need answers to whatever is here.

I am forgetting my manners, Emilio. My mind is turning round so quickly. Would you like something to drink while I am reading everything? I do have a very good vintage wine." "That would be good. How did you know?" "Well, I don't know Emilio. It's a big secret. It was too easy so I will tell you. The first time was at the Athens meeting, you and Giorgio were drinking vintage wine, the barman told me, and the second night was the same, apart from the little misunderstanding with Tullio and Eva, maybe that is why you were both avoiding Eva and myself talking to those secretaries.

Did you find out all the information from them, Emilio, or was it Giorgio, or did they extract it from you boys? Then at the delegate's dinner on the ferry, the girl you were seated next to, both of you were drinking vintage wine." "Ah yes, the ministry secretary, a very good conversationalist." "Yes, she is, and she is also my friend, so she told me everything later." "Giorgio was right. Women notice these things." "Yes. He would know, wouldn't he?"

"Emilio, I know you are hard to all of these sorts of things but also thoughtful and kind, you know me well enough for me to explain what happened." Emilio listened. Francesca had been glad to see her brother again. It had been several years since they last met. There was the occasional telephone call. Francesca spoke, "He then appeared several months ago befriending me when all the time he was working for himself against everything I have worked for my whole life. Even worse I read copies of old documents Giorgio had in his bags. I now find out my so-called blood brother was the illegitimate son of a friend of my fathers, who was supposed to have been adopted by the family. My parents took him in caring for him as their own but the so-called adoption was never made legal. My father only did it to save his then business partner from ruination.

He saved his reputation, practically losing his own marriage by lying and deceiving my mother. It is a very cloudy background that surrounds this story, and to top it all, I then came along much to my mother's joy. I am totally and utterly gutted my whole life, no one told me anything. I am in the right business. You can never trust anyone, my own family especially. I have worked hard trying to restore the families fortunes again. They have betrayed me. I know they always wanted a son but this; there lies the hypocrisy from their high and lofty positions in our society. They deserve the hardships, taking all I have, pushing me to marry wealth." "Oh Emilio. You have a lot of patience." "It's all right, Francesca. Please go on."

"Well, I was being constantly pressured by Antonio and Eva from the very first, using my position to gain access to various buildings and offices, but Giorgio listened to me throughout everything, he started to see the truth. Giorgio, with his crazy plans, was the only one who in the end was the only one to trust, and he is on the other side. Why… why… why is this world so crazy, we do the best we can? And I think I have far too many feelings for Giorgio I should not, what can I do?" Francesca leaned on Emilio's shoulder sitting straight up again realising what she was doing. "I am sorry," apologising to Emilio, "it's so unprofessional; please pass me my bag Emilio. It's at the back of your chair." He passed it over. Francesca found her tissues. Giving a big sigh she dried her eyes. For several minutes, they sat neither speaking.

"Emilio, can I ask you a personal question?" "Try me Francesca as long as you won't be offended by a big no." "Will you and Giorgio ever return to your ship or other ships? Giorgio will never say but you know him, he is your friend." "Francesca those days have gone with most of the people we knew, from casual to close. Pictures we have seen or taken tell stories as reports, letters and poems love and loss. We all have these things in our lives. We have been too many places, and we have done much and seen so many things good and bad. Our days and life at sea are no more for both of us."

"I ask because it is something that Giorgio said to me about a ship, which I think makes him sad. He quoted part of a poem to me—about the ship holds your life." "Ah, I know this, one of two great poems, Francesca, about our late commander, his ship, our lives on the ship, penned by his wife and one by Giorgio's then fiancée Laura. All that happened then to this day is still kept under a dark veil. There was no service to remember old friends." "Does Giorgio have the poem? No, he has told me he never carries it, before you ask I don't carry it. So much happened in a relatively short space of time. We were both there. She was a fine ship.

One month after an incident at sea, we and several other officers moved on to a converted navy ship using our recent experience to assist several communication specialists from London, commissioning their new equipment. It was our final tour before moving to a shore testing station. Sometime later, our old ship joined others on night manoeuvres, probing deep water. She suffered a catastrophic failure." "Oh, Emilio. I'm sorry. I will not repeat what you have told me. I understand a little more about Giorgio, you also Emilio, not returning to that way. Emilio, is there another poem." "No other of the ship, ah the poem to Giorgio, you know this poem, Francesca." "No, you said two great poems, Emilio." "It is nothing. The poem was about the first ship Giorgio and I were on. It was personal from his fiancé, when Giorgio became control coordinator spending too much time away from her, only Giorgio would have this copy."

"Francesca, I should tell you now as we have this time to talk. Giorgio is aware of my position. I requested this assignment to see all went well throughout his journey. I know his ways, which can be unorthodox as you now know, others have referred to it as the nelson touch, this is why we have been able to stop one unauthorised approach towards Giorgio regarding his original assignment. As we unravelled the conspiracy, your position became tenuous we, Giorgio and I, were to see you safely to your destination as discretely as possible at whatever the cost. We have the same very high official contact, who knew someone was manipulating others from the start; you were both used to flush out the moles, it worked but at a physical and personal price on both sides."

"What has happened on the train and our talk will never be repeated. My job is not over yet. I will see Giorgio through to Cannes. On my return from Cannes, I am instructed to watch over you Francesca for a further ten days unless internal changes occur. Everyone will know the truth by then, all will be good. This will be the last timeI see you in such a way. I wish you well whatever you decide to do. It is all for your ears only. I will see Giorgio in the restaurant car and let him know we have spoken. Shall we say one hour? It will give Giorgio and me time to clear up all the loose ends of what has taken place and to pass on to you for your control department. I take it, you will be free to see Giorgio by then, or would you like to leave it to later?"

"No, it will give me time to reflect on what has happened and prepare my report for our arrival to Rome. Thank you again for everything Emilio. Please tell Giorgio I shall be there in one hour." Francesca held Emilio for a moment and stopped. "Oh, I'm sorry Emilio. I am not thinking. Are you still in pain from the shot?"

"No, I'm ok, Francesca. The hug made me feel better. I will make Giorgio laugh when I tell him you injured me with a bear hug. Goodbye Francesca."

✳✳✳

After a change of clothes, putting the details that she had on paper and putting all the documents back in the attaché case, Francesca stood in front of a big mirror on the closet door, thinking I will have to do, before leaving for the restaurant car. She entered stopping by the door looking at Giorgio sitting alone in the empty dining car at one of the middle tables, writing as Emilio had said, probably details of the day's events. She walked towards him. Giorgio stood in the isle looking at Francesca. It was all too much for Francesca. She ran to him, throwing her arms around his shoulders, tears streaming down her face. They stood embracing each other. Giorgio trying to placate

Francesca's fears and anxieties of this traumatic journey. The sudden come down that all was well and now at an end and everyone that mattered to Francesca was all right. Giorgio sat Francesca down at the table and sat next to her. She held his hand and turned, kissing Giorgio on the cheek. "I feel calmer now, Giorgio. It's been such a big impact on me, that bastardly Antonio trying to kill you Giorgio and Emilio. It has made my heart heavy with grief and unhappiness, if anything should have happened to you or Emilio."

"Thank you, Francesca. He hugged her tightly. I don't have a tissue for your tears, but if I put my hand on your cheek, it will absorb them all for me to save and remember." "Giorgio you have a well-hidden romantic side to you." "No, I haven't. It's just to make you feel better, so we can get on with this repor,t and I can have a couple of glasses of wine to forget what I've just said." "Giorgio," Francesca sat up straight. "I don't believe you. It's not true what you have said, is it?" "Of course, it's not true but it made us both perk up." "Oh Giorgio. You're very bad. I should say something, but I don't know what. I shall kiss you for now but I shall think of something later." "Ok Francesca, until then we can read each other's reports before I collapse of exhaustion."

They went through all the events again leading up to the present. Writing up any differences in their own reports that Emilio and Francesca had written earlier. Giorgio handed his report to Francesca, "That's it. What a report, a fine and almost well-structured written document, a real piece of art. any anomalies punctuation will be taken care of by one of the secretaries as always, but will they buy our written account of what has happened, all those faceless shadows of bureaucracy who know nothing of what it's like to be out in the field." "Now, Giorgio, they like to see things all tidied up without any ripples regardless of a few little changes, which we both agree on, so you can look at mine and alter yours. Giorgio, I saw that look. You know what I mean. Just alter yours to match mine; it's only three items, and I have highlighted them for you. When you've finished, I think, it might be time for us to rest."

"Francesca these changes are hardly worth noting. Anyway, why do I have to alter my report?" "Because Giorgio mine has a better presentation about it, so hurry up it's getting late." "Oh, women, can't live with them, can't live without them. Look what about this part, you haven't mentioned the damage to the metal-lined attaché case." "It's not essential Giorgio, and I wouldn't live or sleep with you anyway." "Ok Francesca. I shall be finished in six or seven minutes. then I'm going to stretch out on this bench seat and sleep." "No, you're not Giorgio. When you finish writing, we shall go back to the compartment, where there are two bunks. You need to stretch out and sleep comfortably." "You can have a glass of wine or coffee, before you turn in. Francesca you remembered. Of course I did I always what you say to me. OK I'm finished Francesca let's go to your place Im about ready for keeling over and before you say anything, I will. Dont say any more tell me in the morning Giorgio

"Yes Francesca, It's a good job I'm tired." "Mm," she said as we entered the compartment closing and locking the door behind us. Coming up to Giorgio's side, she turned him round. "Giorgio so there is no confusion, that's your bunk." She pointed her finger. "There's mine." She turned him again, running her finger down his cheek. "Don't forget. Would you like a drink Giorgio?" "No," as he put his note pad and papers on the table. "I would like to climb into my bunk, seeing you won't sleep with me." Giorgio kissed Francesca on her smiling cheek, climbed on the bunk, falling asleep as soon as his head hit the pillow."

Francesca looked at Giorgio for a moment or two, before putting a cover over him, tucking it under his chin. With her hand on the other side of his face, she kissed him on the cheek, pressing her own cheek against his, whispering, "Good night Giorgio." She moved the reports to one side of the table, noting the comments Giorgio had made on his report pad. She sighed, shaking her head slowly looking at Giorgio again as she got changed in to her nightgown, and checking everything was packed away ready for their arrival. Francesca stretched out on her bunk turning to check on Giorgio before turning of the light. And then pulled the cover up under her chin. They both woke at the sound of a train whistle.

The Rome express was approaching its destination. Francesca recognised the surrounding area. "Giorgio, we will be arriving in about fifteen minutes. I am just going to wash and freshen up." They were both ready as the train entered the station, slowing to a stop. The platform soon became very busy, with passengers spilling out and into the station concourse, porters moving quickly and efficiently with trolleys filled with bags.

Chapter 10

Rome

Francesca turned to Giorgio, "Rome at last," kissing him on the cheek. "Mm. You need a shave," as she ran her hand over Giorgio's chin. "I don't know why, but it feels very intimate in a rough way," kissing him again on both cheeks. "Giorgio, if you organise the luggage, I will contact the office to update them of all that has happened. It's very early but such good news will spread very quickly. I shall also contact the hotel confirming our arrival to see if something a little more suitable is available after such a journey. We will have help with our luggage, including Antonio's, I organised hotel transport before we left Brindisi."

The hotel which Francesca knew and chose was very elegantly stylish, central to the city. Giorgio was able to check in without problem, albeit it was early and most people checking out. This was probably due to Francesca's call and her influence, hopefully to the good. Giorgio organised for someone to print off three copies of selected documents from the attaché case, and have them sent up with two continental breakfasts—a varied selection of sandwiches, fruit juices and two flasks of coffee. It was to be sent to their suite with the case of complimentary wine and basket of fresh fruit. They were both exhausted after all that had happened. At least, they could relax. The room turned out to be a large comfortable suite. "A room change, Giorgio. We need the best after such a journey."

"Thank you, Francesca. This is just what we need and for all your help. Just Fran, Giorgio, please. You are my friend. You stood by me and very much more." "Ok, just Fran, only when I think of you. But when we are together, it has to be Francesca; it will always be Francesca. It's too beautiful a name to be shortened." "Thank you, Giorgio. I feel you may know me too well, and I don't think I'm explaining too well,

91

what I mean about what has happened." "You don't have to Francesca. We have both been used and survived."

"Giorgio, I need to explain the whole story." Giorgio sat and listened without interruption. "I have to tell you Giorgio. I was told to recover the documents by whatever means, no matter what the consequences, verbal from my Italian chief direct. Or was it, I don't know now. Eva was involved in so much; she gave me the original information as to you, Giorgio, being involved with receiving the documents, which we now know was not true.

Eva was also involved with Antonio. She had received a partial confirmation from her contact in Athens, who was also connected with Antonio. It was Eva who had worked for private sector finances, all very embarrassing for the Athens office, and not easy for my contact. Then, there is Tullio and Antonio. How were they connected? So many questions.

This is something to be cleared up in house, but it was you who eventually cleared it up Giorgio, and it was you who saved Emilio and looked out for me. You with your off-the-cuff plans. When you originally told me, I didn't think this scheme of yours would work, but my argument with Eva set things in motion, although it could have ended in tragedy. "You did well, Francesca. You were the catalyst that brought them down." "Yes Giorgio, but it is all very embarrassing for us. You and Emilio sorted out so much. I was supposed to keep you here for questioning in this very hotel but not these rooms. This suite is very special."

Francesca realised the whole mess on the train and wanted to make amends. It may have gone a little further than she first thought, although she wanted it to. All of this at the behest of her embassy contact. "Giorgio, you haven't said a word. Is everything all right? Did I talk too long? Have I said too much?" "Everything is good Francesca. I was taking it all in. We survived a very long twenty-four hours, and don't forget your intuition to go along with Emilio and myself, that was a big key. Now, we're all here, and you and I are forever locked into this time, no matter where we go." "Giorgio, I am so tired. Are you?"

"I am, Francesca. You organised this suite. Can you tell me where I sleep?" "On the left side of the bed, Giorgio," she said looking directly into his eyes. "Well after your comment on the ferry, when you kissed me on the cheek saying, we have twenty-four hours to Rome, well."

"Today is the tomorrow you thought yesterday would never come."

"Now, it's just the two of us. We can also share the shower. I shall warm it up for us. Give me five minutes." Francesca called from the bathroom, "Giorgio will you wash my back?" They took a long shower together, dried each other and fell asleep in each other's arms on one of the most comfortable beds Giorgio has slept in.

✳✳✳

Francesca woke early, looked at Giorgio, kissed him on the cheek, got up and went over to Giorgio's bags. Looking at them wondering what files and information Giorgio had, she turned, looked at Giorgio and looked back at the bags. I need to check those files, she thought. All the keys are in the locks. She started with the document case. So many files she opened, several most were copies, two were Giorgio's business and expense accounts with cash in a small bag. She emptied the bag, seven thousand US dollars. She put it all back, wondering about the accounts. She quickly found a pen and paper and copied what she needed, moving on to the biggest bag before realising she had already looked through that one on the train. Closing it again, she quickly looked through the last bag. There were more files, one headed personal and sealed. She carefully opened it, slightly damaging the seal. She swore, then quickly looked at Giorgio. He was still sleeping soundly. They were details for a private account with a safety deposit in Rome. She took a deep breath, unable to understand why Giorgio had this account. All the details were in a plastic folder, name account number and password. She looked again at Giorgio as she copied the details, putting the files back carefully and quietly, leaving the clothes on the chair till she had decided what to do with the brown envelope she found in the clothes bag. When Francesca finished, she fully realised that Giorgio was her field counterpart, covering a far bigger area and knew all her contacts, including the early life of Antonio, much more than she realised.

She now knew parts of Giorgio's personal life and his finances. Only one file puzzled her; it was clearly marked Francesca, but it was empty, apart from one sheet of headed note paper of a wine business that once belonged to the family. It had Antonio's name written on it. What does Giorgio know about my personal life?

He knew about Antonio's life and his dubious birth and background, and when and where I was born. Francesca sat on a chair quietly thinking about the empty file whilst gazing at two photographs she had found in the old brown envelope that had been stuck under a flap at the bottom of the bag, with a letter and two folded poems about a ship, Giorgio and Laura. It wasn't the same one that she had discussed with Emilio. It must be the personal poem Emilio had mentioned. She glanced at it again, all the while questioning herself about all that had happened—the files she had just seen, the money she had been paid by the private finance group, her life within the bureau's offices, and Giorgio, all this in just seven days, how could so much have happened.

She decided to put Giorgio's clothes back, putting all the bags back in their place, apart from the envelope with its contents. The letter was a thank you from a ship's commander and of no interest to her. Francesca looked at the poems again titled, 'Golden Pearl' and 'The Empty Bed,' still undecided whether to read them or copy both. Time was getting on. She decided to read them. The Empty Bed was about Laura's life with Giorgio and the other she in his life who always came first, his ship. It was bitter-sweet so deeply sad for her. Francesca, started to read 'The Empty Bed' headed 'by Laura to you Giorgio love always'.

Francesca held the second poem, 'Golden Pearl.' It was very personal about Giorgio's late fiancé. She looked at Giorgio again, looked at the title and began reading.

"Oh Giorgio. How very sad! I'm sorry I read them now." She folded the poems again, putting both in the envelope and placing it on top of Giorgio's clothes bag. She took the photos, placing them on a chair, showered and got partly dressed. She kissed Giorgio on the cheek and went to the mini bar and poured two orange juices. It was now mid-morning. She watched Giorgio sleeping. All was well with the world. Francesca sat on the bed, her head to one side just looking at Giorgio. Willing him to wake up, she kissed him again on the cheek. This time he stirred. She sat back pursed her lips wanting and thinking of him. His eyes opened. Francesca's closed. She sighed with a deep breath.

Giorgio looked at Francesca and into her eyes, before glancing around the room, noting the luggage. He smiled at Francesca. "I know what you're thinking," she said. "But I, well, before I try to explain, and I know you have just woken up but can I keep these two photos." She held them out to Giorgio, then retracted them. "You won't destroy them if I hand them to you," she said. "It's a chance you'll have to take." "Please don't," handing them to Giorgio. "Oh, Francesca. You didn't have to go through everything to find these, but I don't mind, thank you for asking me, but why bother with these old dock photos, just off the ship. I look rough and worn out. Mind you, Emilio took them, and he looked a lot worse. Happy days. Do you want the one I took of Emilio?" "No Giorgio." "Shall I just bin them? You can get a photo of me from your files any time."

"Stop it, Giorgio. It's a personal thing for me. You know that you're teasing me." "Just a little Francesca. You can keep the photos, but the poems, which you have no doubt looked at, I will keep. So, did you find anything relevant to us or dangerous to us?" Giorgio said as Francesca handed him the brown envelope without comment.

"You knew more about the late Antonio than I did. You also have several coded files. I also have the same. We both seem to have everything the same. You slightly outrank me, and you have expensive clothes, which seem to fit you so very well."

"Thank you, Francesca. Compliments are always welcome, especially from you. The duplicate files are between you and I and Emilio, a little security for the future. Anyway, after all you're work tidying and browsing various objects in my luggage, housework I think you call it, we should go through the duplicate files and make sure we both understand all the details and their benefits."

✳✳✳

"Giorgio, we shall take a break. We deserve coffee. Come and help me." She held out her hand. "All these details, Giorgio, I understand their importance and benefits, especially for us here, but for you and your people, it may be better to let these details stay in your filing system. Maybe one days, they will be useful, but they are very dangerous to so many in the finance markets." "You're right, of course, Francesca. They cover your section mostly. Your top people would be glad to see all these names. If you're going to pass them on, I had better hand mine on. I will wait one month to make sure all goes well. Emilio will inform me one way or another, but I know he will be your shadow when he returns from Cannes, until he and others have tidied up all the loose ends.

Now we've cleared away all the paperwork, maybe we can both relax. Have you finished your coffee, Francesca? I'm sure you would be much more comfortable sitting over here, save you sitting awkwardly over there." "That's a terrible attempt for me to come over there, Giorgio. I will come over to explain how it should be done. Then in a few minutes, she said laughing, "We can go for lunch. Move over Giorgio. I'm on the edge. You're taking up all the room. You need a woman to sort you out; you're too independent."

"Francesca, look at the time. I'm starving. We've missed lunch, and it's time for afternoon tea or an early dinner. You and your few minutes. Come on. There's no more time for playing hide and seek." "You're a spoil sport, Giorgio," Francesca said grumpily. "All right a ten-minute cuddle, then you can wash my back in the shower and repair any damage you've inflicted on it. Are you ready Francesca?" "I'm ready and waiting for you Giorgio. Shall we go for dinner?"

✳✳✳

As they lay in their double bed, Giorgio kept thinking how the time had gone so quickly. The hotel turned into a real haven for both of them, although he couldn't help feeling its original purpose was for something a little more sinister. He thought 2 days and he had been packing again. It's been a comfortable suite, a good size, well-decorated, with every amenity. He wondered if he would remember it as it is. At this moment, he came out of his thoughts, realizing he hadn't stopped looking at Francesca.

"You're dreaming," she said. Giorgio smiled at her and her quizzical face; she returned the smile, which lit up her face and her beautiful eyes. "Francesca, your eyes are so open to me. I can see everything, your life, your love, your soul." "No, you cannot Giorgio," she said quietly. "Can you?" "No Francesca," just a little innocent love.

They talked for quite a while about their journey, their time together, the people they knew, their lives, and about her style, which was very London Italian fashion. They sat close, looking at each other, with almost nonstop eye contact. Looking for maybe a flaw or a flicker of a secret, a hint that this was all true, and we were who we say we are, was that a hint of love or longing, if only I knew.

Francesca stared into Giorgio's eyes, looking for or any sign that he would always be here or at the least say he loved her or would stay or return.

"Giorgio, why don't you stay for a few more days?" "It would be so good to stay, Francesca, but I can't. You know I have to be in Cannes tomorrow. It's not easy." "Could we survive here like this? "Francesca, why not travel back with me to Cannes? You could stay a few days." "It is the same for me, Giorgio. I am expected to stay, now all is resolved or close to being resolved." Giorgio held her in his arms as they sat on the edge of the bed.

They completed their packing. She said goodbye to the suite. They made their way to a very busy lobby, where he checked out. Francesca said her goodbyes to one of the managers.

She came over put her arm through Giorgio's, "Come Giorgio. Let's go to the Trevi Fountain. I shall leave my car here. I spoke to the manager who will keep our bags safely in the office, just one of the benefits of my position. We can take a taxi from outside the hotel."

⸺⸻◆⸻⸺

Chapter 11

The Trevi Fountain

It was quiet at the fountain as they stood with others looking into the clear waters; Francesca took control. "Giorgio, you have to make a wish. Come and stand next to me; we can wish at the same time." They both stood looking into the fountain. Francesca turned to Giorgio,"Have you made your wish?"

"My beautiful Francesca! I have passed on two messages." Giorgio looked deep into her eyes; he could almost see part of one reply. "You made me shudder, Giorgio. I would like to know what you said, but I already know you will not say, as with everything else I ask you. And don't reply, just let me have my say, so that I don't have to reply to you. Maybe that is right, I don't know with you, that is why I have not told you mine, although I am sure you know what I wish for."

"Well Francesca. I cannot see your wish in the water, and I cannot see the coins we threw in." "They have been accepted by the powers of the fountain in exchange for a commitment that I return to Rome. Oh, Giorgio would you find me,? Do you think everything will be all right?" "For you Francesca, always." They walked to the far end, occasionally looking into the fountain. "Take my hand, Francesca. We can cross to the other side of the road. It's not so crowded, and we will have a better view to see the complete fountain in all its architectural glory." "Giorgio, I love to see you in such good spirits, like us running across the road holding hands. It makes me want to do silly things, just with you Giorgio."

They decided to have coffee at the cafe overlooking the fountain; it wasn't too busy, giving them chance to talk. They sat with their coffees, Francesca holding Giorgio's hand. "The view is better, the sun reflecting across the water; You should have your own boat, Giorgio." "The things you say Francesca. On my salary, even with a

98

bonus, I couldn't afford half an engine. Would you want to go halves on one Francesca" "It's the same for me." "What with all your family connections and businesses Francesca." "Giorgio, if only it was like you say, but it is not. You could look after me if you had put aside a little amount somewhere." "I would be happy to if you gave up all this and move to Monaco."

"Do you have a house in Monaco, Giorgio, where we could live?" "No, but we could buy one between us. You have Antonio's cash." "I have returned it all with the documents, Giorgio." "With all the costs Antonio incurred on your family, you should have kept it." "I could not Giorgio. It was the right thing to do, Giorgio. We have time for one more coffee. You can treat me to a large coffee and something sweet."

Giorgio ordered as his mind mulled over Francesca's comments. It just didn't ring true. He thought what am I doing? There's something missing here. What really happened to the money? I don't believe she gave it back or did she?

They both sat looking across at the fountain as their two coffees and two multi-layered cakes arrived. He had decided to have the same. Their talk continued mainly about Rome, the arts, and its classical buildings as this was Francesca's home turf. They watched other visitors in groups, families young and old, looking into or just sitting by the fountain. All were busy with their own reasons for being there, maybe the architectural beauty, the atmosphere of it all or just to make a wish, a bit like them.

"Giorgio, we will need to return soon to collect your bags. I locked them before we left just to be on the safe side. Why are you laughing?" "I know you. It is all right for me to look after your keys. Well you know, what I mean. I feel a little foolish now." "Oh Giorgio. I also want to laugh you know. I would always look how well we know one another." "It's our line of business Francesca."

"And yet, we have only known one another for seven days, Giorgio. Whenever I look at your pictures, it will be as you said, for this short period of time, we are locked together for all time. I shall always know you when I look at them. It will be as if you were always here. Giorgio, before we make our way to the station, we shall detour a little site-seeing. I want to keep you here with me as long as I can, you understand."

Francesca squeezed Giorgio's hand, "You are the only one I have given my private address to, please write to me as soon as you arrive. I want to know you are safe. You know how much I want you to keep in touch. You know how I have not been too helpful to my own office, or should I say I haven't been as forward about our movements, with good reason, of course. You understand don't you, the work, our lives, it's just not easy."

"Francesca, I have not been too forward myself, not after the journey we have endured together." "Giorgio, promise me you will let me know when you arrive in Cannes, please. I'm sorry, come on, we better collect your bags and get you to the station." The hotel was a little quieter. Francesca decided to collect her bags as she would be going on from the station. Fortunately, the hotels own transport was available. The driver spoke to Francesca saying he would wait for them at the hotel side entrance, and take them to the station, and take Francesca on from there. Then it dawned on Giorgio, this was someone Francesca knew. Giorgio had seen them together. He was at the last finance meetings in Athens.

Arriving at the station with ten minutes to spare, they followed the porter to Giorgio's reserved compartment, halfway down the platform. All the way from the hotel, Francesca wouldn't be drawn in to anything other than she may be taking a position with improved status and finance. This change came after her talk with the driver while collecting their bags in the manager's office, while Giorgio stood outside at the front desk. All very strange. Giorgio thought I hope that Emilio and D section come up with something. The porter had put Giorgio's bags in the compartment. They both stood almost in front of one another Francesca looking into his eyes. She smiled as she gripped his hand, neither of them spoke, probably just as well as Giorgio was lost for the right words now. He wanted to say much more but he couldn't. "Francesca be careful. I will write, and I will never forget."

"Neither will I Giorgio. Just remember me as we are. Have a good and safe journey. You know how I feel. You have the self-addressed envelope." They kissed holding hands, looking at each other in deep silence, they both know, they will never meet again, their hands part, they have to go. The guard called out to board Francesca stood very still with her hands at her side. On boarding the train, Giorgio turned. They both gave a small wave goodbye.

✳✳✳

Giorgio thought, no matter what, we know facts can still be clouded when it comes to personal feelings. It's something extra to keep under control if you can; fortunately, we all came through ok and on top, this time. Giorgio settled down to the long journey still thinking over the last seven days. This part of the journey is over and completed successfully in as much we're all intact. We can all feel the relief, excepting the thanks and gratitude of various institutions, finance departments even our own section, that side of things are now more or less at an end, but my original journey is still running; it's not over yet until I'm in Cannes. I have learnt again we can never know everything. Giorgio tried to settle in to reading and updating his paperwork, now he could indulge in maybe fifteen minutes of time to reflect with no need to plough through making decisions on thin facts or waiting for details and everything else to catch him up while on the move.

He collected a coffee from the buffet car and sat there for five minutes, looking out over the Italian countryside. It was a clear warm evening. It's a pity other things couldn't be as clear, even though it's the last part of the journey, I should continue to think positive, to an uneventful journey. Emilio was still on the case somewhere on the train. His last jaunt before settling behind his desk again. Giorgio headed back to his compartment. After settling down again, he started his letter to Francesca that the journey was up to now quiet and uneventful as those interested in him were still in Rome. Their controller, the beautiful Francesca, who truly held many secrets, had given something, which he returned whether it had been in equal share he was not too sure yet. As in many businesses, things aren't always as they seem. He could only compare it to business. They are not friends. They are not in a relationship, he wished he knew.

He looked at what he had written, deciding to complete it after their stop at Genoa. He checked the time, saying to himself, five minutes, and almost to the second, a knock at the compartment window, our own code. "Come in Emilio" Giorgio stood as Emilio came in. They shook hands with a good smile from both. "Giorgio, you're looking too relaxed, you need pressure." "You're right. Just send me another Francesca, that should finish me off." They both laughed. "Giorgio, you did well. You've got nothing to think about until we reach Genoa." "Good. I'm looking forward to seeing the reports, and on that note Emilio I shall settle down to hopefully, an hour's shut eye." He woke to his alarm watch. Thankfully he had slept ok, a bit creased in the joints, but a walk to the buffet car and a coffee would put that right. Emilio sat opposite reading. He gave a nod and carried on. All was well.

✳✳✳

The train stopped in Genoa for a short period. Giorgio watched from the compartment window as Emilio made his way along the platform to an open office door, where the company courier stood. He smiled at Emilio. They shook hands. Another friend from the early days, as Emilio had told Giorgio in the past. He had chosen most of the company couriers all from navy connections. "It's all family then," he said. The courier stepped back inside the door, picking up two bags and placed them next to Emilio. They shook hands again, said a few words, and Emilio made his way back with the bags, entering the compartment smiling. "We have all the documents Giorgio. We should check them all now and see if we and D section made it work."

They broke the seals and unlocked both bags. "Giorgio, what's in your bag? Two attaché cases." "The bonus bag, eh Giorgio. This one contains all the document files."

Emilio passed several file packs to Giorgio. They both started checking the contents. "Giorgio, we were right to check the private address Francesca gave you. According to the report, she is living in a very stylish period house belonging to her late husband. The address she gave you she used to live in several years ago until her marriage. It is only two doors down, a good-sized house, but very run down in need of much work. It is a good area of Rome. It ties in with our talk on the train. She is pushing herself at whatever cost trying to restore the family's prestige, and no doubt her own. She would do anything to that end. It was a gift from the gods when this money just fell in to her lap, with further opportunity, thinking you were an easy touch. No offence Giorgio." "None taken. Carry on."

"The proof is all here Giorgio. She was seen on camera in the bank, where she obviously entered your special account name, the number and passwords. She emptied the dummy account first, and your personal house travel account second. She truly meant it, one bag with 10,000 dollars and the rolled pouch with the confirmed family necklace from the first account box and a bag of mixed currencies from the second account box. She must have been in a hurry, in case you didn't really leave. She arrived early morning at the bank, leaving twenty one minutes later with the bags, and got in to a taxi just outside to who knows where. The thank you note you left in the bag must have pissed her off. The very fact it was there addressed to her regardless of its contents, but she still took it. Both accounts are now closed. She has pocketed the lot. Fortunately, not yours Giorgio, 10.000 in US dollars plus another 12.000 in mixed currencies, not very much Giorgio, but I am sorry we even left that amount in, even though it was from one of their own departments. And according to this message from D section, they intercepted several messages from their control, one is showing she turned in all the missing documents from the offices of social learning to her head of department at eleven hundred hours, all names, listed accounts, land deals, all the items we copied. She even handed back the 12.000 in mixed currencies. I bet that hurt but it got what she wanted a written commendation for using her resourcefulness and courage, winning through to recover everything. She was helped by others, etc. She would have cleaned you out if it was as you said that it was your only account. A smooth bitch Giorgio. You have had a narrow escape. You both had something, but it all seems to have been in shallow murky waters."

"It's true what you say Emilio. We play a dangerous game. Of all the files, she looked through the one which must have made her think was her own, which she opened by cutting the tapes that sealed it, only to find it was empty bar for one blank sheet of headed note paper. She must have wondered why and what had happened to the contents, as I was in wonder at its contents, but she wanted more. All this has cleared my mind Emilio. We can move on but it won't take away how we worked together the highs and lows, and the note in the box was a thank you. I also wished her good fortune and future happiness with the recovered necklace. Only you will know the ending Emilio, if you become her shadow for the next fourteen days."

"I am not sure that will now take place Giorgio, with her commendation she will be expected to play a more active role behind a desk; somewhere, they can keep an eye on her." "You're right Emilio. It's all now very complex for their coordinator. I have no doubt much of what has happened will be brushed under the carpet, along with other bodged jobs, which we know about. When we were preparing to leave Athens, Angie told me that we both needed to be careful and vigilant throughout the journey as others were not as they seem. Telling me a story of when she and Lucia were at a conference in Milan, they overheard one of the ministers call Francesca a social siren, saying to all around it was the name that best suited her."

"Forewarned and good planning pushed through by a professional communications department saved the day, and in a bizarre way, it went almost too plan. In just eight days, I survived the siren's ways. And without being tied to the mast, as Odysseus was." "Nice touch of history. Not bad for you Giorgio. I would not feel too bad if I were you. We both survived and learnt much, although I have wondered Giorgio if she was being paid somewhere along the line."

"We will never know, and we have two hours before Cannes, Emilio. Time for a celebratory lunch and a bottle or two of good wine." "You are right, Giorgio. We will drink to your narrow escape and our end of another assignment." "Carrying their attaché cases, they made their way to the dining car, stopping at the steward's area. Emilio leaned in talking to someone. Giorgio heard their reply and you are most generous Emilio. They took a table in the middle of the dining car, with the steward following them with two bottles of wine and two large glasses. He opened both, filling both glasses. Your coffee and assorted biscuits, including the garibaldi biscuits, will be here in a few minutes. He left leaving two menus.

Emilio raised his glass; you make the toast Giorgio. "To all our hidden helpers, including a profitable audacious plan, Andantes Fortuna Juvat." "I'll drink to that Giorgio, and you used that moto on one of our previous assignments." "Yes, and we survived that one as well." "We did, although we both needed one or two medical repairs. Giorgio there are changes happening. Lucia and I will probably move back to Italy, maybe near Rome, and you my friend what will you do, stay in Italy or maybe someone will choose for you, eh Giorgio? Another glass for you?"

One more to go with lunch. I must keep a clear head for the office. With that in mind, Giorgio, we should reflect on the good side of all that has happened, the people we have met, our last section social, what we have learnt and how we have prospered from it, with knowledge and our payoff expenses all in one go, courtesy of all those involved and now departed. Dollars are just so much more convenient Giorgio."

"Emilio, my old friend, you are so right. When we arrive in Cannes and I have cleared my business with the office, I'll sit with my feet up on a balcony, overlooking the Med. I will open a bottle of vintage wine, hopefully all laid on in the room, and the first glass will be to our long friendship and future success."

"I will take that toast myself and to our next job, Giorgio. Giorgio, I think the day's business will be starting soon;

I will contact the office and tell them your arrival time and to prepare everything for you." "Thanks Emilio. They only need me for one to two hours, including coffee, Thereafter, I shall be several days or more, if things go well, recuperating in a very plush hotel suite, giving me time to evaluate the next assignment and any other company business." "By then Giorgio, I have a feeling we will both be happily tied alongside as you put it." "Maybe Emilio, you never know." "We've passed. Nice I can see Antibes; we'll be in Cannes in fifteen minutes. We better make a move. Don't forget your attaché case Giorgio." "Don't forget yours either, Emilio. We definitely earned both." They made their way back to the compartment.

Chapter 12

Cannes

"Giorgio, my job is over now, and I'm still upright. Thanks to you." "I also thank you, Emilio. I know you cleared the way of one or two for me."

"Part of the job, Giorgio, as in our early days."

They both sat sorting messages. Giorgio finished his letter to Francesca. He felt a certain disappointment toward what had happened, even though he knew something would, he couldn't be sure what at the time. It's tragic it should be the money as the whole journey was fraught with financial in fighting, with such a fruitless outcome for those involved. Francesca was in deep with someone in her own section as well as one or two in the private finance sector. Giorgio hoped it was worth it, but it did move her so-called brother out of the picture.

How quick can time go or a memory fade? We don't see it. We can't feel it, but it just keeps slipping away along with everything else, and in this business with many, we know, as often said, we should do this again but never do. Giorgio put the letter in its envelope and left it unsealed, just in case, he should think of an additional final comment. He can post it at the station. There's a post box just outside the main entrance. They arrived in Cannes where a car was waiting. Giorgio's temporary business associate and the driver were on the platform to take his bags. Emilio was already off the train and close to both. He raised his hand and nodded with a good smile, turned back, shook hands saying a few words to both.

They had arrived safely. It was good to know the information Giorgio had was worth protecting this time. Now, he's here, it's all very much an anti-climax to his journey, the Middle East Athens. The unscheduled rerouting via Rome had changed many things, everything, except one, the realisation that had been hidden somewhere for one person. He looked at the driver as he walked down the platform and wondered about the priorities of his day, and in particular, his associate who was further down the platform. The driver must have been another ex-navy friend for Emilio to know him as he did.

He shook hands with him. He gave Giorgio a friendly greeting, handing him the familiar sealed envelope and taking his bags to the car. Giorgio looked at it thinking, already I've only just arrived, is there no rest for the wicked.

Giorgio opened the envelope studying its contents. Turning to Emilio, Giorgio saw that familiar look of so it starts again as he put the message in his jacket. They nodded to each other. Emilio gave Giorgio a broad grin. Giorgio returned the same as he thought of all the meticulous planning to this journey. He turned and started walking down the platform, carrying his attaché case, heading in to the main station area and straight across through the crowds and out through the main entrance. Stopping next to the post box, taking the envelope from his jacket pocket, looking at it again, made him think of their time at the fountain, their wishes, the train and the hotel. He had only written half a page, but when he put it in the pre-stamped envelope on the train, it had made him think of Francesca's words. The way she said it, the look in her eyes, and send it to my private address. It was safer by post with all the electronics surrounding them. There was nothing to add. He sealed it as he stood next to the post box thinking of everyone he had met in just eight days. He looked at the letter again, her handwriting, the address, and thought 'should I send it? I had promised.' He looked out through the main entrance over Cannes and the Mediterranean. It was calm, with several small boats in shore and a cruise ship further out. He thought of the new message and its content again. It never ends, always a new horizon and whatever hides beyond it. He posted the letter. It was now part of the past and could never have been more. In another eight days where will we all be he thought, as his beautifully disguised associate, Angie, came over. "Giorgio, your car is across the road, forth down on the left, in the short stay zone. The driver will take my car which is behind it. I will take you to the hotel and check everything is in order." Giorgio turned to see the car and driver waiting for Angie to confirm all was well. Giorgio turned back. "Angie you knew, didn't you?" "I'm always here for you, Giorgio. You know that." She took his hand saying, "Come on. We have got a world of things to do." They looked at each other. Giorgio holding her hand a little more firmly, replying, "You're always right, Angie. We have."

The End

The Mysteries of Rome and Intrigue

From the desert sands to Athens and plans,
From that ancient city to the ferry by train,
As our allies discover,
The dangers of another.

As they travel by ferry for another train,
They meet Francesca, a beautiful name,
She is a snare to this bizarre affair,
They travel together, though not a pair.

Just your side, just their side,
They all know but still hide,
What they do they feel it's true,
The loss by train, it's not a game.

Through the night, they exchange information,
Before arriving at Rome Central Station,
The Rome Express, a wondrous name,
To such a now - dangerous game.

Now in Rome, almost safe almost clear,
Both at the fountain of love and dreams,
The sun glows, the water gleams,
Quietly, they think, today is the tomorrow,
They thought yesterday would never come.

Francesca now hates this game,
As she now discovers,
The machinations of others,
Giorgio has protected her twice,
Her life now never the same.

So they live, at what cost?
In deep silence, they both know,
They will never meet again,
Their hands part, they have to go.

UK Retail Price – £8.99

www.ingramcontent.com/pod-product-compliance
Lightning Source LLC
Chambersburg PA
CBHW072146180726
48291CB00008BA/2663